# THE TALL HITCHIN INSPECTOR'S CASEBOOK

## A Victorian Crime Novel
### based on fact

by

Edgar Newman

The Book Castle

Dedicated to my wife
and in memory of Zelda,
whom we both loved.

First published
October 1995
by
The Book Castle
12 Church Street
Dunstable
Bedfordshire

Computer typeset by Keyword, Aldbury, Hertfordshire.
Printed by Progressive Printing (UK) Ltd., Leigh-on-Sea, Essex.

ISBN 1 871199 67 0

The cover design incorporates a detail from a photograph
of Hitchin Market and Corn Exchange c. 1870.
Reproduced by kind permission of Hitchin Museum.

# Foreword

Hitchin is an ancient market town in North Hertfordshire which retains much of its charm despite recent town-planning changes.

In the mid-eighteen hundreds, in which this novel is timeset, it was a quiet, pleasant place of many gracious houses in Tilehouse Street and the curving Bancroft, and a higgledy-piggledy of shops and dwelling places in its other thoroughfares. It did however have an area of slums to the east of its great church of St. Mary the Virgin and these, from time to time, proved troublesome to the police of those days.

In charge of the small local force was Inspector Tripp who stood six feet four inches in his stockinged feet. In this novel, the sequel to *The Tall Hitchin Sergeant*, Tripp, in the course of investigating various crimes, comes into contact with several real worthies who then lived in the town and this provides a slim vein of fact amid what is otherwise fiction.

# About the Author

Edgar Newman was born in the North Hertfordshire town of Hitchin in 1913 and has lived there for most of his life. In 1978 he retired from his post as Head of Publicity and Public Relations for the Potato Marketing Board of Great Britain and turned to writing. A recipe book collated and designed by him sold a quarter of a million copies and his children's crime novel *Bullion and Old Brass* was successfully distributed through a schools' book club. His two Hitchin novels, *The Quack* and *The Tall Hitchin Sergeant*, have both met with much local acclaim.

# Contents

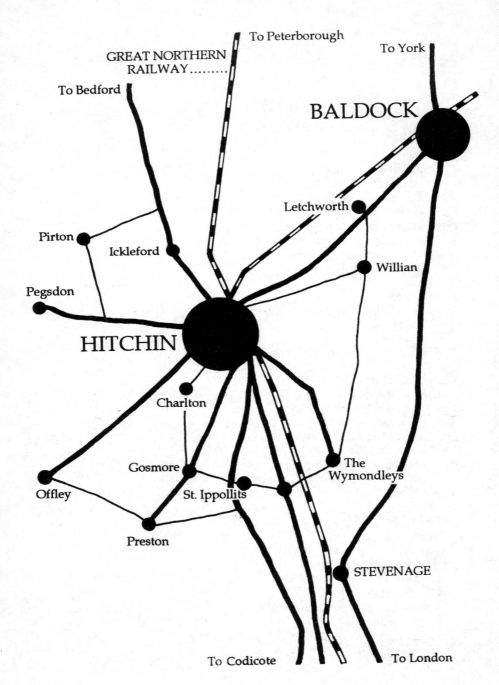

# THE CASE OF THE
# INDISCREET LETTERS

## Dead in a Ditch

It was twenty minutes past midnight and the bells of St. Mary's Church which had merrily brought in the new year of 1866 to the town of Hitchin were being run down in clanging chorus and put to quiet rest in the belfry. The listening Barnabas Tripp, now inspector of police, standing in a pool of yellow light cast by a market square gas lamp, waited for the last of the eight to be silenced before he spoke to the sergeant who had just approached him.

'Right, Pearson,' he said, 'you can stand your men down immediately and get them off their homes and their beds. It's so bloody cold and they're no longer needed here. Almost all of the merrymakers have made off; there'll be no more trouble tonight, of that I'm certain.'

'Very good, Sir,' replied the sergeant drawing his cape more closely around his shoulders and stamping his chilled feet. 'I quite agree, and now snow is beginning to fall in earnest what few are left won't be hereabouts for long, and when they do go they'll be quiet enough. Not that we've had a bad night anyway.'

'What is the tally?'

'Tally, Sir, tally? Well, we've five in the cells. Four drunk and disorderly sleeping it off and one picker of pockets. He's not much more than a boy. We've also stabled one riderless pony. A nice little skewback we found all saddled up and wandering in Pound Lane.'

'You don't know the owner?'

'No, Sir, we don't, but no doubt the little beauty will be claimed tomorrow when someone sobers up and misses him!'

1

Salutes were exchanged as the two policemen parted company and Barnabas, having made sure that his hand lantern was burning brightly, strode off at a good pace in the direction of his home on the outskirts of the town. When he rounded the corner where Cock Street joined Pound Lane the whirling snow, driven by a gusty wind, seemed to be falling even more thickly and he saw it was beginning to coat the ground.

'A foot deep at least by dawn,' he thought. 'No night for any man or any beast to be out in it.'

Although a few windows showed lights most of the buildings he passed were in darkness and it was all very peaceful. For that he was thankful. It was, he hoped, a quiet beginning to another quiet year. This would be his fifth as inspector in charge of the Second Division of the Hertfordshire Police stationed at Hitchin and if it went as well as those which had passed he would be well content. There had been little real criminality in the district and he and his men had been mostly concerned with poaching offences, some petty thieving and the occasional outbreak of rick burning by malcontents.He still had one big problem however; that was the slum area to the east of St. Mary's Church, Back Street and its offshoot yards. Never a week passed without trouble arising there from chronic poverty or brought about by drink or sheer brutality of mind. Damn those who owned the wretched properties and those who ran the dozen or so more beer houses and gin palaces.

A passer by, not drunk but merry with what he had consumed, wished him a cheerful good night and a happy new year and Barnabas, having returned the greeting, felt suddenly uplifted and began thinking of his own happy circumstances. He, and the lovely Laura, had now been married nearly six years. Daniel had been born to them in 1861 and Deborah two years later. They were not wealthy but they had a sufficiency of income. His pay as a police inspector, together with the rents he received from the St. Albans shop property left to him by his late uncle, meant they could live in modest style in the Bedford Road villa he had purchased and now extended by adding two bedrooms.

It was then he chuckled aloud at his thoughts as he battled his way through the snow. If Laura and the children further increased their menagerie and took in more strays or injured animals or birds they would have to consider moving into a bigger house. Now, in addition to Benjy, his black retriever, they had a ginger puss named Joshua, Timmy and Tammy, the grey tabby cats, four white rabbits, three guinea pigs, Barnie, the owl with a broken wing, and a one-legged blackbird. He really should put his foot down and put it down hard when more inmates were being considered. He should, but would he? He chuckled again. It was quite impossible for him to resist three pairs of pleading eyes!

He was still in this happy mood as he drew level with Hitchin's small infirmary on the other side of the Bedford Road he had now entered. Then a soft but grievous moaning noise coming from the ditch to his right brought him to a abrupt halt and he quickly directed the beam from his lantern to where he thought the sound originated. It revealed a man whose body lay half in and half out of the water and whose hands were reaching up in a feeble effort to heave himself on to the roadside.

'Hold on!' shouted Barnabas putting his lantern down in the road. 'Hold on! I'll give you a hand!'

'Trouble, Sir,? Have you got trouble, Sir?'

The voice from behind him was not an unfamiliar one and Barnabas, with much relief, turned to see one of his constables advancing upon him at a run with his lantern bobbing up and down at his belt. When he drew near enough Barnabas saw it was Jennings who had been one of the men on duty in the market place.

'Ah! It's you is it Jennings? Yes, we're in trouble all right. Real trouble! Look at this!'

The constable turned his own lantern's beam on the man in the ditch. 'A drunk, Sir?' he suggested. 'A drunk what's fell in the water?'

'It looks like it. We shall have to get him out and get him home or somewhere dry for the night otherwise he'll soon be dead. He doesn't seem too good even now!'

'No, Sir! 'E certainly don't!'

Jennings put his lantern down close to that of the inspector's and then, kneeling down, tried to get a grip of the man under his armpits with the intention of dragging him up and on to the roadside. But almost at once he gave up and then turned startled eyes on Barnabas. In a shocked voice he said 'I reckon we're too late, Sir. 'E's already a goner!'

'What, Jennings? What? He's dead?'

'Yes, Sir, dead!'

'You're sure?'

'Sure enough, Sir! I 'eard a funny kind of rattle an' then 'e went right limp on me!'

'Well, we shall have to make certain. We can't leave him here, dead or not, so I'll give you a hand we'll get him across the road to the infirmary for a proper examination.'

When, eventually they had carried the sodden body across the road, roused the porter and got the corpse into the infirmary's mortuary Barnabas wiped the mud and what looked like caked blood away from the man's face and then stood back with a curious look on his countenance.

''Ave you recognised 'im, Sir?' queried Jennings.

'I have,' said Barnabas grimly, 'but you won't perhaps. He went through our hands just before you joined us at Hitchin and he's given us no trouble since he was released from prison. His name is Biglow. he and his sister were servants at one time to a certain Zena Tavass who lived at St. Ippollitts and was a quite famous teller of fortunes. Her clients included royalty, so it was said.'

'I 'ave 'eard tell on 'er, Sir, but she's dead now, ain't she?'

'Yes, she died in 1860 and left her cottage and what remained of her fortune to the Biglows. She was an evil woman and she came to a very bad end but they had served her well and she made sure they were well rewarded.'

'An' now Biglow 'as come to a bad end, as well, Sir?'

'He has and I don't like the look of that deep graze on the side of his head. He's been hit by something and I can't believe he just got drunk and fell into that ditch. There's more to it than that, Jennings, much more!'

'Meaning what, Sir?'

'Meaning robbery and murder possibly. His purse seems to be missing and also his hat. He wouldn't have been out on a night like this without some kind of head covering, would he?'

'No, Sir, he wouldn't 'ave.'

'So I shall be most interested in what our Doctor Shillitoe has to tell us when he's had a chance to look at the body later this morning.'

'In the meantime, Sir, what do we do about telling his sister that 'e's dead?'

'Nothing, Jennings, nothing. I'm not prepared to send anyone out to St. Ippollitts tonight with the weather as it is. She'll just have to wait!'

It was nearly noon before Barnabas returned to the infirmary. There he found Doctor Shillitoe still in the mortuary, but he had obviously finished his examination of the corpse as he was washing his hands and arms at the stone sink in the corner and a sheet had been draped over what lay on the stone-slabbed table near the window. Turning to greet Barnabas, towel in hand, he said with a smile, 'This is a fine start to the new year, Inspector, a very fine start you've found for me,'

'In what way, Doctor?'

'Man who's been murdered! Nastily murdered!'

'I feared he might have been but how did he die?'

The doctor hung the towel on a hook near the sink before answering and when he did so there was a twinkle in his eyes. 'It was an acute case of lead poisoning!'

'What?'

Shillitoe grinned as he was helped into his frock coat by the lugubrious night porter who was also the mortuary attendant who had assisted with the autopsy.

'Show him, Billings. Show the Inspector what we found in him!'

Billings produced a small metal bowl from under the shroud and with what was the semblance of a chuckle held this out so that Barnabas could see what it contained, which rattled when the bowl was tipped. It was a lead pellet the size of a big pea.

'There you are,' said Shillitoe, 'a bullet in the belly, or to be more precise a bullet in the liver and he died from a slow internal haemorrhage. He's also got another bullet graze on the side of his skull. That bullet must have hit him hard enough to put him out for a time and he was not necessarily shot where you found him.'

'You mean he could have walked—'

'Or ridden in to get help from someone at the infirmary and then dismounted only to fall into the ditch and fail to reach that help.'

'So we've got a real problem on our hands, Doctor?'

'You have indeed and I wish you luck in solving it. I understand you do at least know who the dead man was?'

'We do but we shall have to get his sister in to formally identify the body, but when it will be possible to do that goodness knows. The road to St. Ippollitts village is under three or four feet of snow so I understand.'

'Well,' said Shillitoe, 'with things as cold as they are he'll keep fresh for a long time.'

'Ah!' added the mortuary attendant with another hint of a chuckle. "E'll keep 'e will?'

## Agnes Biglow Has Much to Say

It was not until five days later that Agnes Biglow was able to get into Hitchin to officially identify her brother's body. A partial thaw and an odd, short, sharp shower of rain had flooded the fields but cleared the roads sufficiently to allow the passage of the pony and trap Barnabas sent to St. Ippollitts to collect her and she and the inspector duly met at the mortuary.

'That's him, that's him all right,' she announced when the

attendant removed the lid of the temporary coffin in which the body had been placed and had then draw the shroud back from the face of the dead man. 'That's Abel Biglow!' Then addressing the corpse she added, 'You silly old fool, Abel, going out on a night like that and getting yourself done in for money we don't really need. I told you not to go, didn't I? Didn't I?'

As she stepped back from the coffin and indicated with a nod of her head that she had seen enough, Barnabas saw her dab at her eyes with the corner of the shawl she was wearing and refrained from questioning her in her immediate distress. It was not until she was seated with him and Sergreant Pearson in his office at the police station that he asked, 'You know, do you, where he went on New Year's Eve? You also know why he went there?'

Agnes Biglow, tight lipped, nodded.

'You do know, Miss Biglow?'

'Yes, I know where he was going and what he was going for. I know all right. It was all to do with them letters he had. He was going to let her have them for five hundred sovereigns and then finish with her for good!'

'What letters, who is she and what about this five hundred pounds. There was no money on him when we found him, nor were there any letters.'

'No letters? No money?'

'Well a little loose silver in one pocket.'

'Strange!'

'Tell me about these letters, Miss Biglow.'

Agnes Biglow hesitated for a moment, then having made up her mind said, 'You know Zena Tavass left us everything she had when she died?'

Barnabas said, 'I had heard so and thought you were both very fortunate.'

'We were, but mind you we had looked after her properly. Well, there were three bundles of letters among the things in a desk drawer. Letters which could make a deal of trouble if they were shown to some people. You know the sort of letters I mean?'

'Indiscreet letters?'

'Indiscreet! That's the word! Silly, lovey-dovey letters that shouldn't have been written.'

'How had Zena Tavass got hold of these?'

'How, Inspector? I don't rightly know but my guess is she bought them off the servants of some of her clients, the gentry that used to come to her for fortune telling.'

'With blackmail in mind?'

'Yes, blackmail, and Abel, when we found the letters, decided to try his own hand at it, Inspector.'

'And did he?'

'He tried but he couldn't trace the writers of two lots of the letters. The third lot were easy. They had been writ by someone local. She'd been paying up regular.'

'Who, poor woman?'

'Lady Brooke.'

'Lady Brooke who lives in Ickleford village at Cadwell Hall?'

'That's her and she's got plenty. She's not poor!'

'I didn't mean poor in that way, Miss Biglow, but poor to be the victim of a wretched blackmailer!'

'She shouldn't have writ the letters then!'

'Have you read them?'

Agnes Biglow smiled salaciously. 'I have! And proper hot stuff they are too! Writ when she was first married but it looks more than like that precious son of hers ain't her husband's and him all high and mighty now he's got that important job abroad!'

'Ambassador in Vienna?'

'Yes. He wouldn't want anything to come out about his wife, would he now, an' she certainly wouldn't want anybody to know what a silly little fool she'd been. That's why she said she'd pay Abel five hundred if he let her have the letters to destroy before they went to Austria.'

'That was quite a lot of money even for her, wasn't it?'

'Yes and she had to ask him for time to sell some rings and things to raise that.'

'He agreed to give her time?'

'Yes, he was agreeable to that and the exchange of the letters for money was to take place on the last day of the old year in the place where he usually collected money from her.'

'Where was that?'

'In that broken down old barn near the entrance gates to Cadwell Hall.'

'I know the place, know it well' put in Sergeant Pearson who had been listening open mouthed at what was being said. 'I know where she means.'

'Good, Sergeant, we must have a good look in that barn to see what we can find and I must have a discreet word with Lady Brooke to see if the appointment was kept.'

The sergeant nodded his agreement and Barnabas turned again to Agnes Biglow saying, 'We shall try to find out exactly what happened and who it was who shot your brother although to be honest I've very little sympathy with you or him. One thing I would like to know is how he got to Ickleford that afternoon. Did he have a conveyance of some kind?'

'He was riding our pony and the pony hasn't come back.'

'Is he a skewbald?' asked Pearson sharply.

'Yes. Three coloured. Rags, we call him!'

'Do you now? Then put your mind to rest on that matter, Miss Biglow, because we've got him safe and sound in our stable. He was found wandering loose in the streets on the night of the day your brother was killed. When you go home today you can take him with you.'

'Thank you, Sergeant, thank you very much, and thank you Inspector for what you're doing.' Agnes Biglow rose from her chair to add 'I know Abel was doing wrong but I want his murderer caught. Caught and hanged!'

'I expect you do, Miss Biglow, and we shall do our best to arrest whoever it was that shot him but as to hanging him that's a matter for judge and jury to decide upon, not us. Not us, thank God!'

The woman sniffed rather contemptuously at this and then said angrily, 'That's a lily-livered answer, that is, Inspector. All murderers deserve to be hung when they're caught!' With this she swept out of the office with Sergeant Pearson close upon her heels. Barnabas, when she was scarcely out of hearing, muttered aloud 'And if all murderers deserve to be hanged then, Madam, all blackmailers deserve to be shot!'

## The Baronet's Lady

Less than an hour after Agnes Biglow's departure from the police station Barnabas was at the door of Cadwell Hall in Ickleford, only to be told by the butler who had answered to his knocking that Sir Henry Brooke had left early that morning for the Continent but that Lady Brooke was still in residence.

'It is Lady Brooke I really wish to see,' said the somewhat relieved inspector.

'Then,' replied the butler, 'I will see if it is convenient for her to receive you.'

It was and Barnabas was taken through to the library where a handsome, dark-haired woman who he thought to be in her early forties, was seated close to a cheerfully blazing log fire. She was not alone. Standing by her chair was an elderly man with a neatly pointed white beard whom she introduced as Colonel Fairfax.

'My father,' she explained, 'and as he will be in charge of the estate in a few days' time when I leave to join my husband in Vienna and you, I expect, have called in respect of the poaching matter we reported, I thought it best that he should be present at this meeting.'

Barnabas, now a little nonplussed, shook hands with the colonel and while doing so was invited to partake of tea round the fire.

'Delighted to do so, ma'am,' said Barnabas.

'Then give your hat and your cloak to James, please, and draw a chair up to the fireplace.'

Whilst a tea trolley was being wheeled in and tea and small sandwiches served, only pleasantries were exchanged and

Barnabas learned from Colonel Fairfax, to whom he had taken an immediate liking, that while it had been a good year so far for partridges, pheasants were very scarce.

'The bag on our big Boxing Day shoot was most disappointing,' said the colonel, 'as it was only two and a half dozen brace! Poor sport for sixteen shooters! And it's those damn poachers who are to blame! I'm damn sure of it, Sir, damn sure! Excuse me a moment while I get the game book from the gun room and you'll see, Sir, how the bags have fallen off over the past two years. Figures don't lie, they don't!'

Fairfax, indignant and red of face hurried out of the room and Barnabas, when the door had closed behind him, immediately said, 'But it isn't poachers I've come to see you about, Lady Brooke, it's a much more private matter and as it concerns you personally I have been waiting to have a word with you.'

Lady Brooke's hand went to her mouth and she rose from her chair.

'Concerns me, Inspector, concerns me? A personal matter?'

'Yes, very personal. I think you've been troubled by a blackmailer, a man by the name of Biglow, haven't you?'

The face of Lady Brooke was suddenly drained of colour and she murmured a quiet 'Yes' to his question.

'Then you will not be sorry to hear that Abel Biglow is dead.'

'Dead?'

'Yes. Dead! Murdered in fact! We found his body on New Year's day!'

Lady Brooke began to sway and Barnabas quickly reached forward to prevent her falling heavily to the carpet. She was unconscious in his arms when Colonel Fairfax returned to the library and gasped 'What the devil is this?'

Barnabas said 'I'm afraid I've given her something of a shock and she passed out on me. Help me please to get her on that sofa.'

Fairfax, demanding no immediate further explanation, did as he was asked and then called for three of the servants to assist their mistress to her bed. He also sent a groom to fetch a doctor.

It was not until a quarter of an hour later, when the colonel and Barnabas were seated together in the library, that Fairfax asked what it was that had caused his daughter so much distress.

'I mentioned a matter of extreme delicacy, Sir,' said Barnabas quietly.

'A delicate matter, was it?'

'Very delicate.'

'One you do not feel able to discuss even with me, her father?'

'As delicate as that. Something very personal to her, Sir.'

'Then, Inspector, I will not press the matter.'

'Thank you, Sir, but I would be obliged if, when you think she has recovered sufficiently, you would ask her if I may call again and ask her a few questions.'

'It may be a day or so before that will be possible.'

'I quite understand. But some assistance with some enquiries we are making would be of considerable help.'

'Then leave the matter to me and as soon as I can I will arrange a meeting with her here.'

On his way back to the police station Barnabas made a point of looking in the almost roofless old barn not far from the entrance gates to the Cadwell Hall grounds. In the rapidly failing light he could just see that it contained a few pieces of rusting iron farm machinery and several bales of damp and rotting straw which smelt foully. In a corner he found a man's hat.

He picked it up and took it to the door opening to examine it more closely. It was sodden. One side of the crown was badly scored. It looked like damage by a bullet.

'So,' he muttered, 'you were here, Master Biglow, and this is probably where you were shot and possibly where you were robbed. But who did it, you bugger, who did it?'

He crushed and stuffed the hat into his saddlebag and then rode back into Hitchin in a very thoughtful mood. Who had got the letters? Who indeed had got the letters?

# Trapped !

Three days were to elapse before Barnabas received a note from Colonel Fairfax suggesting that if he now cared to call at Cadwell House he would be give the answers to all the questions he might wish to ask. The inspector immediately took the police station pony and trap and drove over to the yellow brick mansion in Ickleford convinced he would be able to clear up the mystery of Abel Biglow's death and perhaps, with luck, be able to lay hands on the murderer.

It was, he noted, two o'clock by the tower timepiece as he hitched the pony's reins to the post provided near the front door steps. His summons at that door was answered not by the butler but by Fairfax himself and it was the colonel who took his cloak and his hat before, with these in his hand, he led the way through the hall to the library.

There was no sign in the room of Lady Brooke and at the look f enquiry on the face of Barnabas the colonel said, 'Elizabeth? She is not here, I'm afraid. She had to leave early this morning for Vienna!'

'But it was her I wished to question. It was most important that she was here to give me the answers!'

'Do not worry about that, my dear Inspector, all your questions can be answered by me in full. I can assure you of that so do please sit down and join me in a brandy and do have one of these excellent cigars.'

Barnabas sat down reluctantly in one of the fireside chairs and looked rather nettled. 'This, Colonel,' he said, 'is not a social occasion but an official one! A very official one!'

Fairfax smiled pleasantly. 'I am aware of that, Inspector, but do please make it as enjoyable as possible. These really are good cigars and the brandy is a vintage one. My son in law is a dull fellow but something of a connoisseur when it comes to the good things in life! He really is!'

Barnabas began to relax and took a cigar from the proffered box. He then watched with interest as the brandy was poured into gently warmed glasses.

When both men were settled comfortably in their chairs with the cigars drawing satisfactorily Fairfax said quietly, 'It is not my daughter, my friend, who can tell you best about the death of that wretched man, but me.'

'You, Sir, you?'

'Yes! Me! I shot the bastard! Now let me tell you exactly what happened.'

'Do, but please remember what you say will be taken down and may be used against you. You understand that?'

'I do. Perfectly. But I have no intention of being brought to trial. No intention whatever so your warning is of no consequence. None!'

'We shall see about that, Colonel, but carry on. Do please carry on, do.'

Fairfax gently eased some ash from the tip of his cigar into the silver tray on the table beside him and then asked 'How much do you know of this blackmailing of my daughter?'

'Quite a lot, Sir. We know the blackmailer was in possession of some foolish letters written by your daughter and that a fairly large sum of money was to be exchanged for these at the ruined barn near the entrance gateway to the grounds of this house. This transaction was to take place during the afternoon of the last day of December. Biglow was supposed to be meeting your daughter there.'

'That is correct, Inspector, but Elizabeth did not keep the appointment. I did! That morning she had come to me in great distress and told me everything. But she was in a very nasty predicament. She had not been able to raise the full five hundred pounds he was demanding and she was fearful of the consequences of not being able to pay him. She was sure he would go to her husband with the letters.'

'So?'

'I took the four hundred sovereigns she had acquired and managed to add fifty of my own to these hoping that I could do a deal with the bugger on her behalf.'

'Did you meet him?'

'I did. We met at the time and the place arranged and do you know what he did when I produced the money I had?'

'What?'

'He laughed in my face! He held up the letters and said even the five hundred wouldn't be enough. He wanted six! Now Sir Henry was to take up that wonderful post in Vienna a scandal involving his wife was not to be though of, was it? Six hundred! Not a penny less!'

'Bastard!'

'Yes, Inspector, he was a bastard so I pulled a pistol I was carrying from my pocket and shot him!'

'And you thought you had killed him?'

'I did. He seemed dead enough when he dropped to the ground so I covered him up with loose straw after taking the letters he was still clutching in his hand. I intended to return later when it was dark to dispose of the body.'

'And how were you going to do that?'

'I was going to drop it down the disused well at the back of the barn. It's deep and half full of water.'

'What about the pony? He'd ridden over to Ickleford on a pony, hadn't he?'

'The pony was tethered outside the barn. I was going to free it and smack it on the rump hoping it would make its own way home.'

'Loose ponies often do. And while you were waiting for darkness I suppose you came back here?'

'I did. I burnt the letters and then went to see my daughter in her room. All I told her was that I had got the letters and destroyed them and that she had no need to worry any more.'

'You did not tell her that you had shot Biglow?'

Fairfax shook his head. 'No, I did not. I saw no reason for doing so and I didn't.'

'What happened later?'

'I went back to the barn with a lantern,' said Fairfax, 'but the body had disappeared. So had the pony. I could only assume that I hadn't killed him and that he had come round and ridden off.'

'He had. He had ridden off making for the Hitchin Infirmary

with the intention of getting medical help. He nearly got there only to fall in a ditch on the opposite side of the road. That is where, Sir, we found his body and now, Sir, I must arrest you for his murder.'

'I don't think you will, Inspector, I do not think you will!'

Barnabas found himself being confronted by a smiling man firmly holding and pointing at him, a deadly looking pistol with a double barrel. He said, quietly and without a tremor in his voice, 'Put down that gun, man, put down that gun at once!'

'That, I shall not do. I should be loath to kill you and I shall regret it if I have to do so. I've taken a great liking to you and I wish we could develop our friendship but I've no intention of going to the gallows for killing that wretch. Nor do I intent blowing out my brains. I've planned another course completely.'

'And what is that, pray?'

'A quite simple way. First I shall provide you with a written confession to the murder so that you will need to make no further enquiries which might involve my daughter. Secondly you will provide me with time to make a good start on my escape route.'

'Impossible! I cannot do that!'

'I know you can't willingly do so and I have made arrangement accordingly!'

'What arrangements?'

Fairfax said with a chuckle. 'These! I shall leave you locked in this library for a while. The window is barred and the outside shutters closed and padlocked—'

'The servants will know I'm here!'

'There are no servants in the house! They have all been given two days' leave of absence and none of them are likely to return until the day after tomorrow! You'll be quite comfortable here and you won't go hungry. If you look at that table by the wall you'll see it's covered by a cloth. Under that cloth is food in plenty left by the servants for me. There's a nice cold fowl for you to cut at, cheese, pickles, bread and a dozen bottles of beer. In the cupboard there are plenty of logs for the fire, some blankets and a bucket with a lid which you'll certainly need.'

'You won't get away with it, Colonel, we will get you eventually.'

Again Fairfax chuckled. 'Yes, I shall. I've the money I didn't pay over to Biglow and in the past days I've been able to transfer sufficient funds of mine to a bank abroad so that I can spend the remainder of my days in reasonable comfort somewhere where the sun shines more often than it does in England. Somewhere where the wine is good and life can be very pleasant indeed.'

'You make it sound a most attractive place, Colonel, but it must have its snags somewhere.'

'I don't doubt it but I can see none at the moment and so, taking your pony and trap, I'll set off on my way. I shall be leaving them at an inn near Hatfield railway station where they'll be looked after until you arrange to have them picked up.'

Fairfax, with the pistol still pointing firmly at the broad breast of Barnabas, rose from his chair and backed to the door. Barnabas also rose from his chair but made no threatening move.

'I'll not offer to shake hands with you,' said the colonel. 'That would be foolish on my part but I will wish you well and hope you will be comfortable. The confession I promised you is, by the way, under a plate on the table. Enjoy the remainder of the brandy and the cigars!'

Moving slowly and carefully and never for one moment taking his eyes off Barnabas, Fairfax seemed to slide out of the room. The inspector heard him give a final chuckle as the door closed behind him and the key quietly turned in a well-oiled lock.

Moments later Barnabas, having in vain tried to open the window or the door, helped himself to another brandy and then settled down in a chair regretting his foolishness in leaving his office without telling Sergeant Pearson or anyone else where he was going.

'You, Barnabas Tripp,' he said aloud to himself, 'have been a complete bloody fool and now you must pay the price of your folly.'

He was however released from captivity only twenty-four hours later when the butler, returning unexpectedly early from a disagreeable visit to a disagreeable sister, passed through the hall and heard knocking on the library door. He unlocked and opened this to be confronted by an irate inspector of police.

Back at the police station where a full scale search had been set in motion, Barnabas recalled the searchers immediately and set Sergeant Pearson and two constables to hunt down Colonel Fairfax. He was traced as far as Dover where it was reported he had embarked for Calais.

'He's got clean away' reported Pearson on his return to Hitchin. 'He's shown us a proper clean pair of heels, he has, and I reckon that's the last we'll ever hear of him!'

Barnabas had smiled wrily. 'I dare say it is but them of course, you never know,' he said. 'You never can tell, can you?'

In May, a letter addressed to Inspector Tripp, was received at Hitchin police station bearing a Greek stamp and a crude Athens cancellation mark. The contents were brief. The writer hoped that the inspector had not been too badly inconvenienced by his enforced stay in the library. As to himself he was now happily settled down on a small but pleasant island where he had bought a small vineyard. Regards were sent and the letter was signed by John Fairfax.

Later in the day of its receipt Barnabas showed the missive to Laura. As he handed it to her he said, 'This should interest you. Remember that business at Ickleford village with a certain ex-army officer early this year?'

'Remember it? Shall I ever forget it. Of course I remember that dreadful day when you disappeared! Is the letter from Fairfax?'

'Yes it is. It's quite short. Read it, my dearest, read it.'

Laura, having done so, handed it back to her husband with a smile. 'So,' she said, 'the wicked flourish and it doesn't look as though he will ever be brought to trial.'

'I don't think I want him brought to trial!'

'You don't?'

'No, I don't. Quite frankly I don't think he did kill Biglow.'

'But you have his written confession! If he didn't do it who did?'

'That daughter of his!'

'Lady Brooke? She shot him and took the letters?'

'Yes. I'm convinced that he's covering up for her. She must have gone back to the house from the barn and told him what she had done. He offered to hide the body but when he reached the barn there was no body to be found!'

'Not until you found a body near the infirmary?'

'Yes. How a badly wounded man got so far we shall never really know. When I told Lady Brooke we were looking for Biglow's murderer it must have come as a complete shock to her and of course later, after she had spoken to her father, he knew he must act quickly if the daughter he loved so much was to escape trial.'

'So he has taken all the blame on himself?'

'He has. And so far as I am concerned it can stay there.'

Barnabas, without a qualm, dropped the letter into the fire and watched it flare for a moment before he broke up the charred remains with the poker.

# THE CASE OF THE
# HERMIT'S RING

## The Hermit's Blunderbuss

Laura Tripp, like the wives of most of Hitchin's business and professional men, had long since gone over from serving an early evening main meal to serving what had become known as lunch at, or soon after, noon each day. This arrangement suited Barnabas well. He was able to partake of this repast daily except on Mondays when he rode out to inspect the outposts of his command and had a bite, as he put it, somewhere along the road.

'And no bad thing either,' he had said to Sergeant Pearson. 'No bad thing at all. If I went home on Mondays what should I find? There would be my Laura, Lottie our maid and the weekly laundry woman all glaring at me, the dank smell of washing about the house and nothing on the table except cold meat! No, it's better I should be out and about on wash days!'

Pearson had grinned and nodded sympathetically. He too had no great liking for Mondays and a line of washing in the garden.

At about one o'clock on this Monday in mid May, a grey and chilly one with a touch of rain in the wind, Barnabas dismounted from his horse in the yard of the 'Plume of Feathers' in Little Wymondley village, bear Stevenage, and handed the reins to a waiting ostler prior to entering the inn in the hope of getting a good, hot meal. The innkeeper, Joseph Cotton, a retired army sergeant, was an old friend of his, and his wife, Marie, was a Frenchwoman and a superb cook.

It was Marie who greeted him so warmly when he ducked under the door surround to cross the taproom floor to call out

'Service!' in a loud voice when he reached the bar. In a moment she was out of her kitchen to grasp him firmly and kiss him on both cheeks.

'My Barnabas!' she exclaimed. 'You 'ave come to eat with us again today, I 'ope.'

'I have, Marie, I have. Indeed I have!'

''Très bon!' I 'ave for you something special today. You 'ave I 'ope the good appetite?'

'I have, Marie, a very good appetite! What is it that you are about to serve me?'

'Un cassoulet au confit d'oie!'

Barnabas looked puzzled and Joseph Cotton, who had just appeared from an outhouse wiping his hands on a coarse towel, grinned and said 'A stew of goose, pork and haricot beans cooked French peasant fashion with plenty of herbs and spices. You'll really enjoy it! I'm sure you will enjoy it! It's good! Really good!'

'Très bon!' insisted Marie and then went on with a voluble outburst which the innkeeper, with a smile, translated as, 'I'm to serve you no ale but good red wine and we shall be joining you at table!'

'I'm delighted,' said Barnabas, 'delighted!'

The casserole was as good as had been promised and the full-blooded red wine served with it was much to the liking of Barnabas. As he wiped his platter clean with a morsel of bread he looked across the table at Marie and said, 'Madam, I must congratulate you. It was magnificent! Magnificent! He would have said more, much more, had not a roughly dressed man rushed into the room and across to the corner table at which the three were seated.

'Pleece, ain't yer?' he demanded of Barnabas.

'Yes,' replied Barnabas and what do you want with the police may I ask?'

'It ain't me wot wants yer. It's 'im! Yer wanted over at Redcoats Green you are! Mad Lucas's place! The 'ermit's got 'is bloody gun out an' blazin' away with it at any poor sod 'e can see from 'is winder! Even me an' my mate!'

'And you are?'

'We're is bleedin' keepers. Us wot looks after 'im!'

'What's gone wrong? He doesn't usually make a lot of trouble, does he? If a man chooses to live alone and in filth and give gin and money to tramps and sweets to children that's his business and there's nothing we can do about it. However when it comes to shooting with a gun that is completely different. Why is he doing it?'

"Ad a ring stole, 'e 'as! 'Is mother's ring it was. 'E let a kid try it on 'er finger as she stood by 'is winder. One of the tramps wot was waitin', a red-headed bugger, snatched it off 'er an' ran off with it. I weren't far off but I weren't quick enough to stop 'im, I weren't, an' 'e got away! Mad Lucas is real mad. Madder than most times, 'e is!'

A thought struck Barnabas and he asked 'Did he send you for us?'

"Tween shootin' 'e shouted out somethin' like fetch the pleece so I got the pony out an' started out fer 'Itchin but when I was passin' the ostler sed you were 'ere so I came in. I don't need to go further, do I?'

'Yes, you do! You can go to the police station and get me some help. I'll give you a note!'

Barnabas hastily scribbled a few words on a sheet of paper provided by Marie and gave this to the man. Having done so he called for his horse and found the landlord was also mounting up.

'I'd better come with you to Redcoats,' said Cotton. 'He knows me better than he does you and I ain't scared of him, well not much!'

Not sorry to have the sturdy landlord with him, Barnabas set off and led the way to the hermit's dwelling. He was appalled when they entered the approach drive and saw how neglected the garden and grounds had become. Hemlock, deadly nightshade, nettles and briers were growing everywhere and over everything. It was none other than a howling wilderness of noxious weeks and untrimmed bushes. The house, when they came in sight of it, had a dejected and neglected look about it. What had once been a pleasant residence was now little more than a ruin with its doors and all but one of its downstairs windows barricaded by great baulks of timber. Half the tiles were missing from the roof and the outbuildings were in a state of collapse.

'Crazy, ain't it,' said Cotton as they dismounted some fifty yards short of the building. 'Proper crazy, ain't it? A real madman's bloody house!'

'Yet some say he's not as mad as he makes himself out to be.'

'He's mad all right, Barnabas. He was mad even before that Miss Amos rejected him and married the Hitchin vicar. He was even worse when his mother died and he wouldn't let 'em bury her for weeks, he wouldn't. Worse still when he stripped himself of his clothes and took to wearing nothing but a blanket! Holds it together with a skewer, he does!'

'Thank 'eaven yer've come.' The voice from the nearby bushes was gruff but relieved. A tough looking man emerged warily. "E's quiet for the moment but yer can't trust 'im, yer can't. Charlie fetched yer, I 'spose. Yer've been quick.'

Barnabas nodded. 'I was in the village. You're the other keeper, aren't you?'

'Yes. 'Arry 'All's the name and me an' 'im looks after 'im between us. 'E ain't much trouble at all usually. All 'e wants is 'is eggs an' milk, 'is bread an' 'is cheese an' a 'casional 'erring or two when 'e fancies 'em. We gets 'im sweets for the kids and gin for the tramps. 'E 'ands out the sweets an' the gin from 'is winder. 'E loves kids, 'e does, an' if they 'olds their 'ands in for 'im to kiss, 'e gives 'em sixpence!'

'He's got money, then?'

'Plenty of that, guv'ner. 'E's rich. Stinking rich! They send money over to 'im from a bank in 'Itchin an' 'e gives most of it away to tramps an' kids but 'e ain't giving much away terday, 'e ain't!'

'He's had a ring stolen, hasn't he?'

'Yes, an' he wants it back. Reckons it's a pleece matter. I'll give 'im a shout an' let 'im know yer 'ere if 'e don't already know.'

Waving a piece of dirty white material tied to a stick Hall went forward a few paces and called out, 'Mr Lucas! Mr Lucas! It's 'Arry 'All! Don't shoot! Don't shoot!'

A dark, bearded face, surrounded by a great name of black hair appeared at the one uncovered window on the ground floor together with the muzzle of a blunderbuss. In a pleasantly modulated voice came a reply, 'Is that a policemen you have with you, Hall?'

'Yes, Mr Lucas, from 'Itchin!'

'He can come forward. I'll speak with him.'

To the relief of Barnabas, the blunderbuss was withdrawn from sight and to his astonishment, when he reached the window, he could see that the hermit was smiling at him most pleasantly.

'So I see from your badges of rank, Sir, that you are an inspector of police. I'm honoured, Sir, honoured. Not a constable, not a sergeant but a full blown inspector to see me, yes?'

'Yes, Mr Lucas. I am Inspector Tripp and command the local division. We've not met before, Sir, and although we've never met before I've heard quite a lot about you.'

'Yes, Inspector, I am well enough known hereabouts and even some of the swell mob in London come and see me. Even that writer man Dickens has been to call. Not that I've much time for him. The man's a fool. Thinks I'm insane and I don't like what he has written about me. Do you think I'm mad, Inspector?'

'Mad, Sir? That's not for me to say, Sir. I'm a policeman, not a doctor, but we can't have you firing off your gun at people, can we? Someone might get hurt.'

Lucas laughed. 'But no one has been hurt because what shots I have fired have been well over people's silly heads. It's got me what I wanted, of course.'

'Which is what?'

'Quick attention from someone well up in the local constabulary! You!'

'Because you've had a ring stolen?'

'Yes! And I want it back. It belonged to my mother and it has a sentimental value. I'm quite prepared to give a twenty pound reward for information leading to its recovery.'

'Then, Sir, I'll have notices to that effect printed and circulated. Perhaps you'll describe the ring to me?'

'I will. It's a simple gold band with three small sapphires set in it. Pretty but of no great intrinsic worth.'

Barnabas made a note in his book and while he was doing so Lucas turned his attention to the innkeeper who had come up to the left of the inspector.

'You're Cotton aren't you? You keep the Plume of Feathers in the village? My servants get their ale from you?'

'Yes, Sir, they do. Sometimes they call and sometimes I bring it over here for them.'

'Yes. I've seen you. They tell me you were a sergeant in the army.'

'I was, Sir, Twelfth of Foot, Sir.'

'A fine regiment, I've been told?'

'Yes, Sir, the best!'

'And you're married to a Frenchwoman who is a good cook?'

'I am, Sir. A very good cook!'

'Then get her to bake me a pie. A meat pie. I've a great fancy for one. French flavoured of course. Herbs and spices and I don't mind a touch of garlic.'

'It shall be done, Sir. You shall have it tomorrow!'

'Good! And she shall have a golden guinea for her trouble. Now tell, me, Cotton, how did you come to be with the inspector today?'

The innkeeper hesitated in his reply and Barnabas said, 'He came to support me, Mr Lucas. I was just finishing off a meal at the *Plume* when we heard we were wanted here. Cotton offered to come with me.'

'And to face up to my gun, Inspector? He's a brave man indeed.'

'I've faced up to worse, Sir,' said Cotton. 'I faced the French guns at Waterloo, I did, and them did need facing. So did their soldiers when they advanced on us with their bayonets at the ready. I were only eighteen them, I was, and I was so scared I—'

'Ran away?'

'No, Sir, I shat myself!'

'And I don't doubt,' said Lucas, 'if I had been there I should have done the same!'

Later, when Barnabas and the innkeeper were riding off down the drive of Elmwood House they passed several tramps and one or two children making for the hermitage.

'Amazing,' said Cotton. 'Real amazing!'

'What?' asked Barnabas. 'In what way, amazing?'

'How quick the news gets round that Lucas is now all right again and it's safe to go up to the house once more.'

'Goodness only knows but in my view he wasn't really dangerous and never will be.'

'Hm!' exclaimed Cotton doubtfully. 'Dangerous or not I shan't be taking chances when I deliver that pie tomorrow!'

It was not until he was nearing Hitchin on his way to the police station that Barnabas met Sergeant Pearson and two constables on their way to assist him at Elmwood House. All three carried guns.

'So we're not wanted, Sir?' said a relieved Pearson.

'No, you're not, thank God. All is peaceful again at the hermitage and by now the gin will be flowing once more for the tramps with the sweets and money being given to the children. All that is left for us to do is to recover a stolen ring. If we can do that we shall have a very happy hermit!'


## A Ring For Rosie

Alice Higgins, the slut of an alewife, who kept *The Swan With Two Necks* at the top end of Tilehouse Street, opened the scullery door for the first time that morning to view with disgust what lay in the tiny cobbled yard beyond. There, face downwards in his own vomit and curiously still, was the red-headed, red-bearded man who had got himself so drunk the night before buying drink with the money she had paid him for the ring she was now wearing on a finger of her left hand.

'Get up!' she shouted loudly. 'Get up and get out! Yer ought ter be sober enough by now, yer did! Get out!'

The man made no move and Mrs Higgins went over to him and kicked at his legs quite viciously. Getting no response she pushed at his head with a booted foot to see it roll to one side sufficiently enough to reveal one pale blue eye open and staring vacantly into space.

'Gawd!' she exclaimed. 'Yer dead yer bugger! Bleedin' dead yer are. Choked yerself ter death yer 'ave! Sod yer an' sod yer agin!'

Entering the house she went to the foot of its narrow stairway and called out, 'Aggie! I wants yer quick!'

A girl's voice responded immediately.

'Yes, Ma!'

'Are yer dressed?'

'Nearly, Ma!'

'Good! Yer'll 'ave ter go down ter the pleece station an' tell 'em.'

'Tell 'em what, Ma?'

'We've got a dead 'un in the yard an' they'll 'ave ter deal with 'im, they will.'

When, a minute or so later, the girl had taken a quick look at the body, retched and joined her mother in the scullery she said, ''Orrible, ain't it? Real 'orrible! Ain't 'e the man what got 'is 'and up yer skirt last night an' yer 'ad term slap 'is chops?'

'The same!'

'You'd just give 'im twenty-five shillin' fer that ring yer wearin'?'

'I 'ad. An' then I got most of it back fer the gin 'e bought fer the lot what come in an' 'imself. But don't yer say nothin' about that when yer sees pleece!'

Aggie, who by now was tying her bonnet ribbons under her chin grinned and shook her head quickly. There was a cunning look on her face when she said, 'Not bleedin' likely, Ma. Not bleedin' likely. The less I tells 'em the better. That ring was maybe stole an' they'll take if offen yer, they will. No, I shan't say nothin' I shan't.'

Aggie was scarcely out of the street door when her mother took the ring from her finger and gave it a rub on her apron. She had already made up her mind about what to do with it. She would sell it and she knew who would probably buy it from her. Rosie Linden one of the two sisters who lived almost opposite, was fond of pretty things and could afford to pay a good price for it. The two women were well off. Not only were they good, skilled straw plaiters but they had a highly profitable sideline. Yes, she would offer the ring to Rosie, and Rosie, she was sure, was not likely to ask any awkward questions.

It was Sergeant Pearson, assisted by Constable Jennings, who dealt with the body in the yard and arranged for its removal to the mortuary. They also set in motion the arrangements for an inquest and the burial at the expense of the parish.

Questioned by Barnabas later in the afternoon Pearson said he had thoroughly searched the body and discovered nothing by which the man could be identified. Although he fitted the description of the man who had robbed Hermit Lucas, no ring had been found.

'He had three shillings and fourpence in his breeches pocket but nothing else, Sir, nothing at all.'

'Have you had a word with any others of the tramping fraternity?'

'Several, Sir, they knew him as Red Rufus. They said he was a bit of a loner.'

'Make a few more enquiries, Sergeant, and try the workhouse. He might be on the register there.'

'I will, Sir.'

With that the matter was dropped at the police station but in a Tilehouse Street cottage that evening Rosie glanced with pleasure from time to time at the pretty ring, now adorning her little finger, which she had bought from Mrs Higgins. She was sure she had a bargain. She had paid three pounds for it.

Tomorrow that nice Mr Melton, who repaired clocks and watches and jewellery at Mr Gatward's shop in the Market Place, would be called upon her for his pleasuring, and she would then ask him to value her purchase. He was a man she could trust implicitly.

## Rosie Returns the Ring

Oliver Melton was a small, shy man but one so bountifully endowed by nature Rosie had been amazed when he first revealed to her the magnificence normally concealed by the broadcloth of his breeches. That afternoon of the day following her purchase of the ring, after she had twice pleasured him to their mutual satisfaction, she waited for him to adjust his dress and then asked him what the ring she was showing him was worth.

'Not that I'm wishful of selling it, Mr Melton, I'm not, but I've thought it would have cost a deal more than I paid for it if I had bought it from Mr Gatward's shop.'

Milton took a small magnifying glass from his waistcoat pocket and began to examine the ring carefully. Almost immediately, with the glass still screwed into his right eye, he stopped and turned to her saying, 'Dear me, Rosie, did you know this is stolen property?'

'It's what?'

'Stolen property! It fits exactly the description of a ring the police are looking for and they have circulated all jewellers and pawnbrokers with a notice this morning. How did you come by it? Pray tell me.'

'I bought it off Mrs Higgins who keeps *The Swan With Two Necks* across the road. I paid her three pounds for it!'

'Well it's worth a deal more than that and there's a twenty pound reward offered for its recovery!'

'Twenty pounds!'

'Yes. Twenty pounds! You must tell the police at once and

claim the money.'

'I shall! Do you know who it belongs to?'

'Yes. Mr James Lucas!'

'Mad Lucas? The hermit of Redcoats Green?'

'None other. One of those tramps who call on him for gin and money snatched the ring away from a child who was being allowed to look at it.'

'How did Mrs Higgins get it? Do you know?'

Rosie told him.

'And the tramp is dead?'

'And you gave the Higgins woman three pounds for it?'

'I did!'

'Well you look like making a handsome profit on that deal, don't you?'

'I certainly do, Mr Melton, I certainly do!'

Rosie did not take the ring into Hitchin police station until the following morning. Then, she and her sister, both fairly discreetly dressed and with light make-up, presented themselves at the counter of the outer office and asked to see 'That nice Inspector Tripp.'

Barnabas being free at that moment, they were ushered into his presence by a young constable who regarded them with wide open eyes and mouth agape when the inspector rose from his chair and greeted them warmly with 'Rosie! Ruby! And what may I ask brings you here? Do please sit down.'

They sat and then Rosie, from her reticule, produced the ring and gently put it on the table in front of Barnabas and said, 'I'm told you're looking for this!'

'We are certainly looking for a ring which has been stolen from Mr James Lucas and what you are showing me does meet its description. How did you come by it?'

At the conclusion of her story Barnabas grinned and said, 'In view of that all that's remaining to be done is to give the ring back to Hermit Lucas and collect the reward money from him. I suggest we do it now!'

'Now?'

'Yes, Ruby, now! I've a fairly free morning and you two have a hired pony and trap available so we can set off almost at once for Redcoats Green.'

So it was that it was only a few minutes later when Barnabas led the way out of the police station yard with the pony trap close to the heels of his horse. Sergeant Pearson, watching the small procession leaving, chuckled and said to himself, 'I guess you'll have a tale to tell, Guv'ner, when you get back. I sure do reckon you will have. A proper tale!'

It was a pleasant journey meandering through white blossomed lanes at a gently ambling pace. Barnabas was in nor hurry to get back to his desk and was enjoying the fresh air and the sunshine.

It was Ruby, at the reins of the pony and trap, who, as they rounded the first bend in the drive up to the hermit's house, said, 'I'd heard things were bad here but I didn't think they could be this awful!'

'And I've just got a first glimpse of the buildings.' said Rosie, 'and they all look as though they're ready to fall down. Fancy, a gentleman with money choosing to live in a place like this!'

As Barnabas dismounted from his horse and the pony trap was brought to a halt at the front of the house, Lucas,s two minders emerged from their hut in what had once been a rose garden. The one Barnabas knew as Harry Hall came over to speak to him.

''E won't see nobody terday. Nobody, 'e won't. 'E's got the sulks proper, 'e 'as. Right proper!'

'He'll see us,' replied Barnabas. 'We've got his ring!'

'Have you now?'

The voice came from behind the bars to the window of the hermit's cell and his bearded face appeared. 'Have you now? Then I will see you, Mr Inspector, so come close.'

'I will.'

'And who are the women in that trap?'

'The lady who recovered your ring and her sister.'

'They're no ladies! They're whores. I can tell a whore a mile away and they're whores!'

'And you're no gentleman,' said Rosie. 'No bleeding

gentleman at all or you wouldn't be calling us names!'

'Touché!' The hermit was smiling, white teeth gleaming amid the beard. 'I apologise. And which one of you ladies has my ring?'

'I have!' declared Rosie holding the ring up so that Lucas could see it. 'And for twenty golden sovereigns you can have it from me!'

'Ten!'

'Twenty!'

'Fifteen!'

'Twenty! That's what you offered and that's what you've got to pay!'

'All right, twenty, you strumpet, and you'll have to tell me how you got it. Earned it on your back, I've no doubt!'

'No, I didn't. I paid for it!'

'Tell me more!'

Rosie told him all and Lucas laughed.

'So he choked himself did he, on his own vomit?'

'He did!'

'Good! Serve him right! Are you going to share the reward money with the alehouse woman?'

'Not bloody likely! Why should !?'

'You would if you were a lady!'

'I don't pretend to be a lady! The last thing you called me was a strumpet! So I'll be a strumpet!'

Lucas grinned and then disappeared from the window to reappear moments later with a small leather bag in his hand. He held this for Rosie to see and called out, 'Bring the ring over to me. You and you sister both come!'

Standing close to the window the sisters could see into the dimly lit cell and realised the floor was knee deep in cinders from the fireplace and littered with broken crockery and other rubbish. The rising stench was vile.

'Hold your open hand out, woman,' said Lucas to Rosie.

She did so and the hermit counted not twenty but twenty-two sovereigns into it.

At her look of enquiry Lucas added, 'Two for that woman

Higgins.' Then looking at Barnabas he went on, 'And you, Inspector, make sure she gets it!'

'I shall,' said Barnabas who to his astonishment saw that the hermit was definitely ogling Ruby.

'And here's three for you, woman,' he said softly. 'You buy something pretty with them. I've taken to you, I have. Really taken a fancy to you!'

'Have you now?' replied Ruby taking the money from him, 'but I ain't got a fancy for you and I couldn't get one even if you offered me two hundred pounds. You're ugly and you're dirty and you stink of stale piss and worse! You're horrible, real horrible.'

Lucas's smile gave way to a fierce grimace of rage as he stepped back from the window. Withdrawing the skewer from the dirty yellow blanket enshrouding him he allowed this to fall at his feet to expose his complete nakedness beneath.

'That to you, woman!' he snarled, 'that to you!'

The three close onlookers stood for a moment in silence and then Rosie, having slowly eyed the nude hermit up and then down looked him full in the face and said in scathing tones, 'Well, Hermit Lucas, what of it? You've nothing much there to be proud of! Already this week I've seen better by far. Something to make two of yours and then have something to spare! Yes, to spare!'

Turning about abruptly she led the others back to where the man, Hall, was minding the pony and trap and holding the reins of Barnabas's horse. He greeted the trio with a scowl saying, 'Well I 'opes yer ain't bin upsetting 'im. Yer 'avent 'ave yer?'

'Upsetting him?' said Ruby chuckling. 'We haven't been upsetting him! My sister's just flummoxed him, she has!'

# THE CASE OF THE
# RICKYARD BLAZE

## The Troubled Mr Doubleday

The Hitchin Chess Club met at seven in the evening of the first Wednesday of each month at the Workmen's Hall at the top end of Brand Street. It had about thirty members, among them Barnabas Tripp. The inspector was an enthusiastic and fairly competent player of the game and when, on that July evening, he found he had drawn Mr Oliver Doubleday, the club's secretary, as his first opponent he was more than delighted at the prospect of a hard tussle ahead.

'Well, Sir,' he said, as they sat down to face each other across the table, 'I have a felling that tonight I may be more fortunate than I have been in our past encounters.'

'You do, do you, young man?' replied Doubleday with smiling lips but eyes which seemed troubled behind the thick pebble glass of his spectacles. 'You do? You think you'll get the better of me this evening?'

'Well, Sir, I intend to do so if I can.'

'Then we shall see what we shall see,' said Doubleday quietly, picking up one of the white pawns and, after momentarily concealing both hands behind his back, presenting two clenched fists for Barnabas to see.

'Choose, my friend, choose and discover who has the first move in our battle of the pieces.'

Barnabas lightly touched the proffered right hand to see the fingers open to reveal the pawn. 'I see, Sir, that I am to have that advantage,' he said with a grin as he began to plan his attack. 'A happy omen perhaps?'

They commenced playing but they had not made many

moves before Doubleday lost his queen in exchange for a mere bishop.

'Foolish of me!' he muttered and then made another disastrous move which not only cost him a knight but allowed Barnabas to call an eager, 'Check, Sir, check!'

'That was even more foolish of me,' he murmured as he moved his king to an adjoining square. 'Very foolish indeed!'

'You are not yourself tonight, Sir,' said Barnabas sitting back in his chair, 'Not yourself at all. Are you not well?'

'Well enough in body, Barnabas, but not in mind. I had thought a game or two might help me forget my problems, but this game has shown my thoughts are elsewhere. I must apologise to you for providing an unworthy opposition.'

'Would you like us to abandon the game, Sir? So far you have not been able to do yourself justice. Should I win such a game as this I should only feel it was a hollow victory.'

'I am grateful to you for the suggestion, Barnabas. I am in agreement with it, thank you.'

'And we will have it recorded as a drawn game in the club records?'

'Yes, Barnabas, let it stand as a drawn game and I will now leave you and return home to concentrate on what is best to be done under the circumstances.'

As Doubleday picked up his hat and prepared to leave the meeting Barnabas said, 'These things which trouble you, Sir, is there anything Laura or I, or both of us, can do to help? We will do so happily if there is?'

Doubleday shook his head, hesitated for a moment and then looked intently at Barnabas before shaking his head again. 'Thank you, Barnabas,' he said, 'Your offer is well meant, I know, and I do appreciate it greatly. However I must decline your help. So good night to you my friend, good night. May our next meeting be a more fortunate one and end more happily than this one.'

As he closed the door of the room behind him the watching Barnabas wondered what it was that was bearing down on the old man's shoulders, and later that evening, when he and Laura were preparing for bed, he mentioned the matter to her.

'It can't be money, can it?' she asked pausing for a moment in the brushing of her dark, abundant hair.

'It shouldn't be,' replied Barnabas. 'The Lucas's treated him quite generously when he retired from the brewery counting house a few years back. I'm told that they not only gave him a pension but presented him with the deeds of the cottage he lives in with his widowed daughter and that son of hers.'

'That grandson, Henry Widson?'

'Yes, Henry. You made a face when you mentioned his name. Why?'

'Perhaps it is him who is the cause of the trouble. I don't like the look of him at all and he keeps bad company.'

'Just sowing a few wild oats, Laura.'

'Maybe. But I'm told he's drinking too much and gambling and—'

'And what, my love?'

'You know what!' replied Laura, catching a glimpse in the mirror of her grinning husband towering above her in his ornate night shirt.

'Shall I say it and spare you blushes?' His great hands were resting on her shoulders and she nodded with a smile as she placed her hands over his in a gesture of deep affection.

'Yes! You say it, my dearest.'

'Well, whoring then!'

'Silly young fool, isn't he, Barnabas, when he could settle himself down, marry a nice Hitchin girl and raise a family?'

'Like the two of us have done, my love?'

'Like we are still doing! And I've news for you!'

'You have?'

'I have! I'm pregnant again!'

Moments later she was enfolded in his arms and later still, when they had taken their fill of each other, she went off into a deep sleep, happy and contented.

## A Dishonest Servant is Dismissed

The next morning, at nine, as had been requested in the previous afternoon's note, Oliver Doubleday presented himself at the doorway of the Lucas brewery counting house in Sun Street and was immediately taken through to the general office. Memories came flooding back. There he had risen during his sixty-two years of working life from office junior to the position of managing clerk. There he had made innumerable neat entries in journals, cash books and ledgers and served his masters with great diligence. Little had changed since, with failing eyesight, he had retired four years previously and handed over his post, and the office keys, to the thin-lipped and severely mannered Joshua Covell. Two clerks still occupied the tall stools at the high desk close to the window which would have provided a view of the busy brewery yard had not the lower panes been frustratingly glazed with frosted glass and the office junior still had his cluttered table in the corner with his back towards the clock he was not supposed to watch. Oliver wondered whether the piece of broken mirror glass he himself had used so long ago was still hidden in the table drawer. He guessed that it was and despite the trouble on his mind half smiled.

Covell had risen from sitting at the table on the dais at the far end of the room and he came forward to greet his predecessor as he entered the office. They shook hands and an enquiry was made about the older man's health.

'I am as well as my years permit, Mr Covell, but your note asking me to call this morning to discuss a very serious matter has distressed me greatly. Something Mr Samuel wishes to see me about before he unfortunately has to take certain steps?'

Covell, with his finger pressed to his lips, nodded in the direction of the two clerks and goggle-eyed junior indicating nothing more was to be said in their hearing and murmured, 'Yes, Mr Samuel is expecting to see you as soon as you arrive and I'm to take you straight upstairs to him. Perhaps you would care to lead the way to his office?'

Samuel Lucas, the white-haired and distinguished looking Quaker brewer, business man and part time painter of country scenes, looked up from his desk when the two men entered his room and said, in his quiet, pleasant voice, 'A good day to thee, Oliver Doubleday, although I fear it will not continue to be so for long. It is a bad, sad business which brings you here.'

'Bad and sad, Mr Samuel?'

'I am afraid so.' Lucas picked up a sheet of paper on which had been tabulated some dates and two totalled columns of figures. 'Look at this, please, old friend, look at this.'

Doubleday took the paper and saw that is was headed COLLECTIONS FROM TENANTS AND PAYMENTS TO CASHIER MADE BY HENRY WIDSON all neatly underlined.

'My grandson?'

'Your grandson!' said Covell. 'Yes, your grandson. The young man that you recommended to us for employment as our cash collector!'

'But there is a discrepancy between what was collected and what was paid in to you!'

'There is! A discrepancy of eighteen pounds, ten shillings and ninepence. And we have only checked back for two months!'

'And there is no doubt about the shortfall?'

'None at all. Your grandson has been cheating the brewery. He is a thief, Sir, a thief!'

Samuel Lucas held up his hand with concern plainly written upon his face as he looked at the now ashen visaged Oliver Doubleday. 'Sit thee down, old friend, sit thee down!' he said hastily. 'I know this matter has come as a great shock to thee. It has to me. Place a chair for him, please, Joshua Covell, and help him to it.'

When Doubleday, still visibly shaken, was seated he asked in a tremulous voice is his grandson had been questioned about the matter.

'No, not yet,' replied Samuel Lucas, 'And we have yet to decide what our next step should be.'

'I say we have no choice,' said Covell with conviction. 'We

must call in the police and let the law take its course.'

'That will mean prison for Henry,' said Doubleday. 'His life will be ruined and I don't want that. If I refund what has been stolen and he is dismissed from his post will not that suffice?'

'No! He must be properly punished!' Covell sounded very firm. 'He must go to prison!'

'Hold thee hard, Joshua Covell, hold thee hard!' Samuel Lucas spoke out in a sharply raised voice. 'I too, have no wish to see an old and much loved friend's grandson imprisoned. He shall certainly be dismissed today but as for the money which is missing this can be written off as a bad debt.'

Joshua Covell glared and then murmured in disgust, 'You are being too lenient with him, Sir, far too lenient.'

'Maybe I am, Joshua Covell, but my decision is final and is not to be questioned. Later today, when the young man returns from his round thou shalt bring him to me. I shall then admonish him severely and dismiss him in thy presence. Is that understood?'

'It is, Sir!'

'Then you and Oliver Doubleday may now leave me and get about thy business and I shall get on with mine.'

Waving away Doubleday's attempt to thank him Samuel Lucas picked up his pen and began writing a letter.

At the close of business that evening, immediately after Henry Widson had handed over to Covell the money he had collected during the day, he was taken up to the office of Samuel Lucas and berated by him quite firmly. He was then dismissed from the brewery's service. This despite a tearful and passionate appeal for a second chance.

'No!' said Samuel Lucas, 'Thou shalt not be given a second chance. And let me tell you that you must be thankful there will be no prosecution for theft. Because it would have distressed thy grandfather so greatly the police are not being brought in and you will not be sent to prison.'

Widson's tears gave way to rage. 'Sod you and sod him!' he shouted, 'Sod both of you and you too, Covell! Sod you all!'

'Out!' ordered Covell. 'Out, and stay out, you wretch!'

'Yes! I'll get out!' shouted Widson flinging open the office door with violence. 'I'm going all right but I tell you, you haven't heard the last of me, you haven't! Not by a long chalk, you haven't. I'll get even with you Mr High and Mighty Mister Bloody Lucas. I'll be getting even with you! You see if I don't!'

With that threat Widson ran from the office and clattered down the stairs and out of the counting house.

'And what do you think he means by that?' asked Samuel Lucas.

'Goodness knows,' replied Joshua Covell. 'I'm sure I don't. He'll never be allowed in this building again, of that I am certain!'


# A Fire and a Murder

In September after a brief spell of hot, dry weather a number of rick fires in the vicinity of the Wymondley villages gave deep concern to the local farmers and landowners. Inspector Tripp and his small force of police officers in Hitchin were quickly called upon to deal with the matter and fortunately they were able, within a few days, to lay hands on the culprit. It turned out to be a simple-minded youth living near Great Wymondley church who thought he had heard the voice of God telling him what to do. He was immediately put under restraint by being placed in the care of the county asylum at Hertford.

'And that's that!' exclaimed Sergeant Pearson when he and Constable Jennings reported back to Barnabas on their return from the county town. 'We shall get no more trouble from him, shall we, Sir?'

'No, we shan't,' agreed Barnabas, 'and that's mainly due to your good work on this case, Pearson. You were the one who asked the right questions in the right place and got the right answers to them. I've made a special note on your record sheet to that effect and I shall draw attention to this when the records are reviewed.'

Pearson, a modest man, thanked Barnabas profusely and left the inner office at the police station with a smile on his pleasant face. He was obviously delighted with the commendation and that evening when he reached home he got much pleasure in relating everything to his plump little wife and their plump little daughters.

But early next morning he and Barnabas were called out to another rickyard blaze. This time a big one at Oughton Head Farm, owned by the Lucas's on the north western outskirts of Hitchin.

Although the fire was dying out by the time the policemen reached the scene a great, billowing cloud of smoke and steam was still rising into the grey morning sky from the ashes of the seven great stacks of corn and a barn which had been destroyed by the conflagration.

Having dismounted and secured the reins of their horses to a five-barred gate the two policemen walked over to where a small group of men was gathered near the entrance to the rickyard. This smoke begrimed and weary looking cluster included James Lewin, the brass-helmeted captain of the Hitchin Fire Brigade, the two Lucas brothers, William and Samuel, and a large, rotund man who was introduced by William Lucas as the farm bailiff Simon Yates. 'Lives at the farm, Inspector, and manages it for us."

'And you gave the alarm, I suppose, Mr Yates?' asked Barnabas.

'I did, Inspector, about three o'clock. My wife woke me up. She'd seen the flames through the bedroom window. That son of our rode into Hitchin and called out the brigade.'

'And we got here with the engine and some men well within the hour,' said Lewin, 'but the fire was well away by then and we couldn't do much except save it spreading to the main lot of farm buildings.'

The fire chief took off his helmet to mop at his sweating brow with a neckerchief before adding, 'There weren't that much water in the duck pond and the river is too far off for us to reach it with our hoses.'

'But thanks to you and your men,' said Samuel Lucas, looking up from the sketchbook in which he was recording the dismal scene, 'thanks to you and them, the farmhouse and all but one barn are still intact.'

'It was touch and go, Inspector,' said Lewin. 'Proper touch and go, and in my view it's now a matter for you and your lot to deal with. That's why I sent for you.'

'Arson? A fire raiser again?'

'I'm sure of it! And worse!'

'Worse?'

'We've found a body in what's left of that barn.'

'A body?'

'Yes. A bit charred but recognisable!'

'You know who it was?'

'Yes! Old Betty Belcher,' said the bailiff.

'The woman tramp who hangs about Hitchin?' asked Pearson.

'Yes, Sergeant. She turns up here every year about this time to join our potato picking gang and I always give her leave to sleep in that barn when she's hereabouts. She's a good worker and she must have heard that we'll be lifting potatoes next week.'

'We'd best have a look at what's left of her, Sergeant,' said Barnabas, 'and then make arrangements with the coroner.'

'Yes, Sir,' Pearson replied. 'Whoever set fire to this lot has a bit more to answer for than what he thinks, hasn't he?'

'He certainly has!'

Barnabas and Pearson led the way to the partly burned out barn followed by Lewin, the Lucas brothers and the farm bailiff. It was Yates who pointed to what lay beneath a tangle of charred, fallen roof beams.

'See her?' he asked. 'See that bottle of gin she's still clutching at?' She liked a drop of gin when she'd money to buy it.'

'Are you suggesting, Mr Yates, that she was in some kind of drunken stupor when she was caught in the fire and didn't realise that she was in danger?'

'I am, Inspector. I am! I'm quite sure she was!'

'And I'm not so sure,' said Barnabas.

With the help of the bailiff and Lewis some of the blackened beams were lifted to one side and Barnabas was able to get a really close look at the dead woman's head. Despite the charring it was possible to see she had been struck a heavy blow behind the right ear.

'It's murder!' exclaimed Pearson. 'Murder! She's been murdered!'

'Yes,' said Barnabas. 'Now we've got to find someone who is not only an arsonist but also a brutal murderer. My guess is that she woke up to see someone torching the barn, started to run off to give the alarm and her killer ran after her to hit her from behind.'

'With this!' said Lewin picking up a big and heavy flint stone on which their were traces of grey hair and congealed blood.

'How dreadful,' said Samuel Lucas. 'How very dreadful. Poor woman!'

'Yes, Sir,' agreed Barnabas taking the murder weapon from the fireman's hand. 'Poor woman, indeed. Let up hope we shall quickly find the wretch who killed her. To that end I think we had best leave it to the firemen to retrieve her body while the sergeant and I adjourn to your farmhouse, Mr Yates, and start asking questions. It will be you, Sir, we shall want to question first.'

## The Pointing Finger

As the Lucas brothers wanted to be in on the enquiry it was five in all who sat down round the table in the farmhouse kitchen.

'How many in all do you employ on this farm, Mr Yates?' asked Barnabas, having seen that Sergeant Pearson had opened up his notebook and was ready to record the answers to the questions he proposed putting.

'Twenty-one beside myself. That is regular,' replied the bailiff. 'Fifteen men, three boys and three women. At harvest times we can take up to a dozen more.'

'Do you know if any of them may be bearing a grudge of some kind?'

'I don't reckon so. We treats 'em fair here, we do, don't we, Mr William?' Yates appealed to the elder of the Lucas brothers for a reply to this question and having received a nod of assent went on 'Most of 'em get a little extra in their wages from time to time and there's always a nice little bonus at Christmas time and another one when the harvest is safe home.'

'So you wouldn't expect any one of your regular workers to be responsible for the firing of the ricks?'

'No, I wouldn't, and as for murder there ain't one of 'em capable of it. I'll swear to that. Not one of 'em now!'

'Now! One of them now capable? Have you had someone in the past who might have been?'

Yates hesitated before replying, 'Well, last year we did have a troublesome shepherd we had to get rid of sharpish but he moved right away. Other side of Bedford so I was told.'

'So now there is nobody at this present time who bears you or your employers any ill will?'

'I can't think of anybody. Honest, I can't!'

'But I can,' said Samuel Lucas quietly and regretfully.

'Who?' asked his surprised brother.

'Someone, William, who, when I dismissed him recently for dishonesty at the brewery, threatened to get his own back.'

'Pray, who was that?'

'Young Henry Widson!'

'Old Mr Doubleday's grandson?'

The bailiff said, 'The fellow who used to come our from the counting house each Saturday and bring the wages for the farm workers here. That's who you mean, don't you, Mr Samuel?'

'I do!'

'Then,' said Barnabas, 'we must question him as soon as possible and find out where he was in the early hours of this morning. Does anyone know what happened to him after he finished at the brewery?'

Samuel Lucas shook his head. 'I know not, Inspector.'

'Nor I,' said his brother. 'I hope, though, for his

grandfather's sake, he can clear his name.'

'As Oliver Doubleday is an old and valued friend of mine,' said Barnabas, 'I too hope that Henry Widson is not the man responsible for what has happened here.'

That afternoon Barnabas called at Oliver Doubleday's cottage in Park Street to enquire the likely whereabouts of the old man's grandson. His knock on the door was answered by Doubleday's daughter, a pleasant rosy cheeked woman, who took him through to a back room where her father was playing chess with Schoolmaster Fitch. Both men looked up from the chessboard to greet him warmly.

'I'm sorry to interrupt your game in this way,' said Barnabas, 'but—'

'But—'

'But us no buts, Inspector,' said Fitch, 'your arrival is timeous for me. I am just about to suffer a most ignominious defeat. Look!' He pointed to the board where the black king was trapped in a corner by the white queen and a white rook. 'Hopeless, isn't it?'

'I'm afraid it is,' agreed Barnabas. 'It is indeed a hopeless situation you have got yourself into!'

'And that being so, Oliver,' said Fitch ruefully, 'I have no option but that of resigning! The game is yours and I must leave you to your victory, my old friend.'

The schoolmaster rose from his chair and not for the first time did Barnabas wonder how this fragile looking man managed to rule so successfully over the boys, largely from the notorious Back Street, who attended his school.

'And you will leave your revenge to our next time of meeting?' said Oliver Doubleday with a smile.

'I shall, Sir, I shall!' With that, using his stick, Fitch limped from the room.

When he had gone Doubleday asked, 'And now, Inspector, what can I do for you?'

'Tell me, Sir, where can I find your grandson?'

'Henry?'

'Yes, Henry Widson. I wish to eliminate him from some enquiries we are making. I must see him and question him to do that. Where is he, please?'

A frown crossed Doubleday's face. His voice was tremulous when he asked, 'What wrongdoing has he been up to now?'

'None, I hope, Sir, for his sake, your sake and his mother's sake. But where was he last night and very early this morning? Was he here?'

'Not here, Inspector. He no longer lives here with us. After the difficulty he got into at the Lucas brewery he was dismissed and for a time he was without employment.'

'Then?'

'Mr Joseph Pollard of High Down took him on as a trainee gamekeeper.'

'High Down? That's the big house off the road to Pirton village, isn't it?'

'Yes. A cottage went with the job and we, his mother and I, helped him to furnish it.'

'So he is living fairly close to Oughton Head Farm?'

'Yes. You can just see the farmhouse from the cottage. But what has this got to do with Henry, Inspector?'

'It is possible that he may have noticed something last night. There was a big fire at the farm.'

'Fire? At the farm?'

'Yes. Seven great ricks and a barn were destroyed!'

'But I'm sure he had nothing to do with setting them on fire. He's been bad at times, I know, but he'd never get involved with anything like rick burning.'

'But we would still like to question him. You understand that, don't you Sir?'

'Unfortunately, Inspector, I do but I am sure he will be able to clear himself completely.'

'Yes,' thought Barnabas as Mrs Widson brought in a tray with two cups of tea on it. 'I do hope he can, otherwise two nice people I like very much are going to get badly hurt and sorely distressed. And it isn't just rick burning. There is likely to be a murder charge as well.'

Twenty minutes later as Barnabas was rounding the corner from Bridge Street into Sun Street he saw Sergeant Pearson emerging from the Lucas brewery yard. The sergeant stopped and waited for him to get close. 'Henry Widson, Sir,' he said.

'Yes, Sergeant, and what about Henry Widson? What did you find out?'

'I've just been talking to Mr Covell, the managing clerk in the office.'

'And what?'

'He says young Widson did threaten Mr Samuel Lucas on the day he was dismissed. Made threats in no uncertain terms!'

'So it does seem, Sergeant, that the sooner we have a few words with Widson the better.'

'Do you know where to find him, Sir?'

'Yes. I know where he is supposed to be living. According to his grandfather he has a cottage along the Pirton Road in sight, in sight mind you, of the Oughton Head Farmhouse.'

'Does he indeed, Sir?'

'Yes! And while there is still plenty of light I propose that we ride out and bring him into Hitchin police station for questioning.'

Pearson, grave of face, nodded agreement to this proposal and the two policemen quickened their pace as they hastened across the Market Square and into Cock Street. Within minutes they were saddling up their horses in the police station yard.


## Sudden Death

It was still short of four o'clock when Barnabas and Sergeant Pearson set off on their ride to High Down. With them went the police station's pony and trap with the young constable, Sidney Jennings, at the reins. They had no difficulty in locating Widson's cottage nor his person. He and an older man, both with guns under their arms, were standing by the cottage door in deep and noisy argument. It was so deep in fact that neither of the men involved in it seemed aware of the approaching policemen who heard the older man shout, 'But yer weren't 'ere last night, wos yer, Widson?'

'I was! I was here all night, Mr Cannon! All night I was!'

'Yer weren't, Widson, yer weren't! I knows yer weren't. I knocked 'ard on this 'ere door at three o'clock and agin when I got back at five. I could 'ave done wiv yer 'elp, I could. I couldn't tackle them poaching buggers over t'other side of the 'ouse not on me own, I couldn't. There wos three of 'em!'

'No you couldn't, Mr Cannon, you couldn't, but I didn't hear you knock. I swear I didn't!'

It was at this moment Cannon became aware of the small posse in the road to turn round and call out, 'An' wot do you lot want?'

'Not you, Sir, not you,' said Barnabas, dismounting. 'We need to have a word with Widson there. We too want to know where he was last night!'

'Here! I was here!'

'No yer bloody weren't!' declared Cannon firmly. 'I know yer bloody weren't!'

'I was! I was! I was in a deep sleep. I didn't hear any knocking. As God is my witness. I didn't!'

'You can leave God out of this,' said Barnabas. 'There's been Devil's work around here, there has, so tell me, did either of you see anything of the fire at Oughton Head Farm last night?'

Widson shook his head. 'Not me, I was asleep as I keep on telling, but this morning, when I looked that way, I did see smoke rising and I wondered.'

'What about you, Sir?'

Cannon said, 'I saw the flames when I was knocking at this young bugger's door. It looked bad but I'd got me own troubles, 'adn't I? I'm 'sposed to be larnin' 'im I am an' 'e's 'sposed ter be 'elpin' me. But a bloody lot of 'elp 'e is when 'e's wanted. I've bin lookin' fer 'im most of the day ter give 'im an earful but I ain't laid eyes on 'im 'til just before yor lot come! 'E's bin proper missin', 'e 'as!'

'I've been about,' said Widson. 'Been about like you told me to do.'

'More like bin inter Pirton. Boozin' at the Fox, I bet!'

'No, I haven't, Mr Cannon! I've just been about. Shot a magpie, I have and a badger!'

'Well, I'm not satisfied,' said Barnabas, 'and we're going to have a look round your cottage to see what we can find and then take you into Hitchin for questioning.'

'Questioning about what?'

'A fire and a murder at Oughton Head Farm!'

Sergeant Pearson and Constable Jennings were now flanking Barnabas and the three looked formidable.

Widson, his face suddenly distorted by rage, raised his gun to his shoulder and pointed this at Barnabas.

'You're not taking me anywhere! I don't know anything about a fire or a murder. And if any of you comes closer I'll shoot!'

'Don't be a fool, Widson! Better come quietly man and not make things worse than they are. You'll get a fair trial and if you haven't done what we think you have, you'll get off. You're innocent unless we can prove you're guilty, you know that!'

'Fair trial? Don't make me laugh. I'm not taking any chances and I've no intention of swinging for the killing of some old biddy like her! No intention at all!'

'How do you know it was an old woman who was killed. No one has said who it was! Why did you do it man, why?'

'So you've caught me out, have you? Well I did her in because she saw who I was by the light of the torch I was carrying and I've been about when she's collected her wages. I chased after her and clobbered her.'

'And you thought you were going to get away with that and also get your revenge on the Lucas brothers as you'd planned?'

'Yes, Mr Bloody Inspector, yes! I'm now going to ride off on one of your horses and take the other one with me so you can't follow me. First though I'm going to lock you in the cottage, the lot of you, and don't try anything silly or two of you will get belly-fulls of what you don't want! And I can't miss at this range!'

'Best do as 'e says,' warned Cannon. 'That gun 'e's got is loaded both barrels an' it's 'air triggered. Wot's more 'e ain't safe wiv it!'

It was Barnabas who led the way into the cottage. He was followed by Pearson and then Cannon. Young Jennings who was bringing up the rear suddenly saw Widson's gun wavering for a moment. He took a chance and flung himself at the murderer. There was a loud explosion as both barrels of the gun were discharged and Jennings fell forward to the ground clutching at, in death, what had once been his face.

Widson stared down at the body for a moment, dropped his now useless gun, and then started to run to where the police horses had been tethered. He never reached them. Pearson, erupting from the cottage, was too quick for him and before he could unhitch the reins had grabbed him by the collar of his coat. Within moments Barnabas had joined in the struggle and clapped handcuffs on Widson's wrists.

Later than day at Hitchin Police Station Widson was charged with the murders of Betty Belcher and Constable Sidney Jennings.

The hanging of Widson took place at Hertford Gaol at eight o'clock in the morning of the second Monday in January 1867. Kicking, struggling and cursing he had to be dragged to the gallows. Those he cursed most were Samuel Lucas, Quaker, and Barnabas Tripp, Inspector of Police.

The gentle brewer and artist prayed for his soul at the time of his passing into another world. Barnabas did not. During the night his beloved Laura had been safely delivered of a sister for Daniel and Deborah and his happiness had no bounds, putting thoughts of Widson well out of his mind.

Later that day he did make a point of calling on Oliver Doubleday to see if anything could be done to help the old man and his grieving daughter. Mary Widson greeted him red-eyed from weeping.

'Was the sentence carried out?' she asked.

Barnabas nodded. 'It has been. We received a message to that effect an hour back.'

'Then he is at peace?'

'I trust so, Mary. He has paid in full for what he did wrong.'

Mary Widson murmured, 'God forgive him and be merciful to him. He wasn't all evil, you know, Barnabas, and when he was young he was a good, kind boy. Whatever he has been since, as his mother, I must grieve for him and mourn his end.'

'That is understandable, Mary, quite understandable. But how is his grandfather taking it?'

'Very badly, I'm afraid. He has said little since the trial and spends most of his time sitting at a table and staring at a chessboard. I think his mind has gone. Mr Fitch calls frequently but is unable to persuade him to play a game and the pair of them just sit there silent. Mr Fitch is with him now.'

When they entered the back room the schoolmaster, who was seated opposite to the vacant-faced old man, shook his head sadly.

'There has been no response at all this afternoon, Mary, none at all. He doesn't even seem to see me or hear what I say to him. Somehow I think he knows what has happened this morning but it is impossible to say anything for sure.'

It was then Oliver Doubleday spoke and spoke for the last time in his life. He said, in a mutter, 'I do know what has happened today. Henry has been hung. He has been hanged by the neck until he was dead! He has been hanged! Hanged! Hanged!'

Almost rising from his chair Doubleday fell gently forward across the chessboard scattering the chessmen in all directions. His face, as he fell, became oddly relaxed.

Barnabas went to his side immediately and felt at the scrawny neck for a pulsebeat. Looking up at Mary he said, 'I'm sorry, my dear, I can feel nothing. I'm afraid he's gone.'

'Gone? Dead?' queried Fitch.

Barnabas nodded and Mary Widson began a quiet sobbing.

An hour or so later, after arrangements for help had been

made with kindly neighbours, the doctor and the undertaker, a very subdued Barnabas made for his home. There, Laura, radiant in her own happiness, comforted him and made him pick up the newly born child.

'I'm glad it is another little girl,' she said, 'but I suppose I should have been just as glad if it had been another little boy.'

'And what, my darling wife, are you going to name her?' asked Barnabas looking down at the tiny mite in his great arms.

'Patricia!' said Laura firmly. 'I've set my mind on Patricia!'

'Why, my dear, why? It's not a family name, is it?'

'No, my dearest, it is not but I knew someone once named Patricia who was very gentle and sweet and kind and I'd like our daughter to grow up just like her.' 'Then Patricia it shall be but I insist on having Laura as well. Patricia Laura! I like that!'

# THE CASE OF THE
# MASKED RAIDERS

## The Conspirators

The plan to rob the Hitchin branch of the London and County Bank was hammered out in a dingy, candlelit, room above the livery stable adjoining the Half Moon Tavern at the Bull Corner end of the dismally named Dead Street. The three plotters concerned were Silas Snode, the stocky tavern keeper, his brother-in-law and owner of the livery stable, Richard Bonsey, and Paul Weston. The twenty year old Weston was the son of the manager of the bank they intended to rob.

'It'll be be dead easy if we stick to doing exactly what we've just agreed to doing.' averred Snode, his American drawl distinctly noticeable. 'Real dead easy.'

'But can we go over it once more, Silas?' asked the black-jowled Bonsey. 'We don't want no mistakes, do we?'

Weston nodded. his eyes were bright and his young face flushed with excitement when he said, 'No, we don't want any mistakes, Silas, so do go through it again, please.'

'I sure will if that's what you both want but you'll have to wait while I get myself a draw.' Snode carefully lit a small cigar at the candle flame in the lantern on the table and allowed the blue smoke to dribble from his lips before continuing with, 'The three of us ride up as bold as brass to the front door of the bank five minutes before it's due to close. Me and Paul dismount and hand the reins over to you Dick. You stay up in the saddle and just hold the horses ready and steady while we go into the bank with our shooters. Me with the revolver and Paul with the shotgun and a sack. When we get in he fires one barrel at the ceiling to bring down some plaster and make everybody in there frit for their lives and knowing we mean business. Me? I shouts out and tells 'em to lay on the floor face down and they won't get hurt—'

'Clerks and customers if there are any such?'

'Yes, Paul, everybody in there but you give your sack to one of the clerks and make him fill it from the pile of canvas bags which you say will be stacked at the top of the vault steps ready to be taken down for the night.'

'Yes, Silas. The red bags contain gold and notes in them. The blue with silver money, the green with copper.'

'You make him fill the sack with red and blue bags. Copper you leave. It weighs too heavy for what it's worth. When he has got as many bags in the sack as he can carry, me and you and him back to the door. You and the clerk go to the horses and I stay behind to keep us covered. As soon as you've packed our saddlebags with what has been taken, fire off your remaining barrel and I'll come out and join you.'

'Then?'

'Then we'll ride off at a canter up Cock Street, through the market place and make for Hitchin Hill and the London road.'

'Then,' said Bonsey, with eagerness, 'we part company and circle the town in different ways to come back here at different times to have a share out!'

'We do,' replied Snode. 'We do! We have a share out!'

'Equal?'

Snode grinned at Paul's question. He said, 'Fair shares for everybody. We shall all have taken part in the raid, Dick here will have supplied the horses, you, Paul, have supplied us with the background information and I'm supplying the know-how. So it'll be fair shares for all. Agreed?'

'All right by me,' said Bonsey.

'And by me,' said Weston.

Two minutes later, after Paul Weston had left to catch the train to Cambridge where he was supposed to be studying, Bonsey produced a squat bottle and two far from clean glasses into which he poured two generous tots of whiskey.

'D'you reckon, Silas, we can trust him?' he asked looking towards the doorway through which Weston had passed.

'Young Paul? I guess so. He's a bit shaky but desperate for money. Real desperate.'

'How come? Doesn't he get a proper allowance from his father?'

'Not a big enough one for him to play around with. Like a lot of other youngsters up at Cambridge he's got himself into debt. Into debt with a nasty bookmaker and an even nastier moneylender. The usual reasons of course. Slow horses and fast women but what's worse he's got one of the college servant's daughters in the family way and she's either got to he paid off or married off. That won't please dear papa!'

'How do you know all this?'

'How, Dick?' One afternoon in my taproom he got to drinking too much and when we were on our own he tried to borrow some money from me. I said I was strapped for the ready, which I am, and I couldn't help him. It ended up with him in tears saying that the only way out of his troubles was either to shoot himself or rob a bank and there was one bank in particular he would like to rob! His scrimshanking father's!'

'And that's how this got started?'

Snode took a long swig at his whiskey, wiped his mouth with the back of his hand and grinned. 'It was! I told him if he'd got that sort of idea in his mind and needed help I wouldn't mind joining in with him. I'd seen a bank being robbed when I was living in Texas and it seemed an easy way to get a lot of money quick. All you needed was two or three likeminded men with good horses who were prepared to take a bit of a risk. Quick in and quick out and quick away! It was then he asked me if I'd actually been one of the raiders but I told him that was none of his business. None of his business at all but I was ready to look into the matter and I could bring in a friend who could be trusted and could provide the horses we should need.'

'Meaning me, I suppose?'

'Yes, you Dick, but I didn't tell him you had been with me in the States and we'd ridden with the James brothers a time or two before escaping to little ol' England with enough to set ourselves up here.'

'Just as well, perhaps. I'm still not all that certain about that little bugger Weston but as things are now with trade so bad for both of us we've got to take a chance. This one, with good inside knowledge, looks worth taking.'

'It sure does, Dick, it sure does!'

The eight o'clock train from Kings Cross arrived at Hitchin station a few minutes before nine o'clock each weekday evening to be divided into two parts. The first half setting off for Cambridge and the second half, having been provided with its own engine, eventually departing for every station on the line to Peterborough. Barnabas, who had promised Laura to call at the station and escort her mother off the London train to her home, having been delayed by police business, arrived on the platform just as the Cambridge portion of the train was moving off. A face, dimly seen at a passing window, made him thoughtful and puzzled him. He was sure it was that of young Paul Weston but late that afternoon, when he had met his father at the bank in Cock Street James Weston had said in the course of the conversation that Paul rarely came home in term time and it had been some time since he had last seen his son.

'Strange,' he muttered to himself as he turned his attention to Mrs Ashton and her several shopping bags. Surely the boy must have gone home during the day and his father would surely have known of his presence in the town?

Having seen his mother-in-law to her home Barnabas, by way of a treat for Benjy who was with him, walked the dog up

and over Windmill Hill stopping as he usually did on the crest
of the hill to stare down into the ill lit area of the Back Street
slums. It was then he remembered what Sergeant Pearson had
mentioned to him some weeks earlier.

'Young Weston,' he had said, 'I reckon he's been keeping
bad company this vacation.'

'Has he now?' he recalled replying. 'Very bad? Something I
ought to tell his father about? You know Mr Weston is a close
friend of mine?'

'I do, Sir, and I know he's a very nice gentleman but whether
you say anything to him or not is up to you. All I know is that
young Paul has been spending a lot of time is some of the Back
Street public houses and has even been seen coming out of
Tilly's place.'

'He'll catch more than a cold if he dips his wick in that dirty
oil, Sergeant!'

'Her certainly will, Sir. It will be a nasty dose of the clap!'

But Barnabas had not spoken to the banker about the matter.
The next time they had met Thomas Weston had been full of
praise for his son. The boy it seemed had spent two weeks of
his vacation working in the bank on a training course. He had
been both diligent and hardworking showing quite an aptitude
for banking. The inspector had felt then that it would have been
useless at that time to say anything derogatory about the lad.

Now, having seen Paul Weston returning to Cambridge after
what must have been a surreptitious visit to Hitchin, he was not
so sure about maintaining his silence.

Having put Benjy on his lead a thoughtful Barnabas set off
down the hill for home.


## The Concert

The following morning, after a late breakfast, while Laura was
securing a loose button on his uniform jacket, Barnabas did
speak to her about his misgivings in respect of Paul Weston.

'Am I right in not saying anything to his father?' he ventured.

Laura looked up from her sewing but hesitated before replying. She knew the Westons well. Thomas Weston, the widowed banker, was the honorary treasurer of the Hitchin Symphonic Society of which she had recently become musical director and Weston's housekeeper was a member of her mother's rather select sewing group. His daughter, Sylvia, had been her star pianoforte student at Mrs Bonnamy's Academy for the Daughters of Gentlemen; she was still coaching her and Paul she had met on many occasions.

'His father won't take it well if you do,' she said. 'Paul is the apple of his eye and you really haven't much to go on, have you? Some reported sightings in Back Street and a glimpse of him returning to Cambridge when it was not known he had been to Hitchin. Not quite enough in my view. Not enough.'

'Than I shan't say anything!'

'Good!' Laura having completed her needlework cut off the surplus thread with her scissors and then went on with, 'You'll be pleased to know that we have sold all the tickets for tonight's concert at the Town Hall and Mr Weston has promised his bank will donate five shillings in respect of every pound we ourselves raise by the event.'

'Very generous of the London and County. The Infirmary fund will benefit greatly and you should easily reach the target you set.'

'I'm sure we shall now and Barnabas—'

'Yes, my dearest?'

'Don't you dare be late tonight! I want the full choir in place by twenty-five minutes past seven for a prompt start at seven thirty!'

'Yes, my dear, I shall be there, I promise,' said Barnabas meekly as Laura, on the tips of her toes, helped him into his jacket.

The large concert room at the Town Hall was full to capacity. Everybody in or around Hitchin who thought themselves to be somebody was present in the audience or among the performers assembled on the specially extended platform stage. When Doctor Shillitoe, the chairman and compere for the evening, arrived to take his place at the small table to the right of the stage he did so to a polite murmur of applause which he acknowledged with a twinkle in his eyes and some bobbity bows to his right, his left and centre. At seven thirty precisely he sharply rapped three times with his gavel on the resonant wood block on the table and the hubbub of voices in the room died quickly away into an expectant silence.

Having, in his slightly high pitched voice, welcomed the audience and spoken of the constant need to raise funds for the town's infirmary, he called Laura to the conductor's rostrum. She, after a quick look round at the now standing choir and instrument poised members of the orchestra, swept singers and players off with a down beat of her baton into a lively rendering of Greensleeves. This was followed by the male members of the choir going to sea with a medley of shanties in which the man was well and truly blown down, the drunken sailor put in the long boat until he was sober and fond farewells were sung to the ladies of Spain.

'That was something I really enjoyed taking part in,' murmured Barnabas to his fellow bass as they sat down together in the back row of the singers. Weston grinned to murmur in return, 'I too, Barnabas, but that wife of yours took us through at a rattling fast pace tonight didn't she? We must have raised the anchor in record time!'

'She threatened she would,' replied Barnabas, 'and it certainly went down well with the audience, didn't it?'

Next followed a charming duet rendered by Chemist Lewin's two daughters with this followed by a tall, earnest young man with a pleasant tenor voice singing, 'Drink to me only with thine eyes,' and addressing himself towards Sylvia Weston who was accompanying him on the piano.

'That young fellow seems entranced by that daughter of

yours, Thomas,' said Barnabas softly as the audience applauded the efforts of the now blushing and bowing young gentleman.

'He is,' replied Weston, 'and that minx of mine is not averse to him. To the contrary in fact.'

'He's new to the town isn't he? I've only recently seem him at choir practice and I didn't know until I saw tonight's printed programme that his name is Melton, Maurice Melton.'

'Yes, he is new to the town. He's recently been appointed as a trainee manager at our bank here.'

'Has he, indeed?'

'Yes. His father is one of our principal stockholders, but I'll tell you more later. Your wife has just returned to her rostrum and is throwing some rather quelling looks in our direction I'm afraid! We'd best be quiet!'

Mozart's 'Eine Kleine Nachtmusik' which came next was well received by the audience and well and lengthily clapped. It was followed by an octet of ladies singing 'Jesu Joy of Man's Desiring' at the conclusion of which Laura made an announcement.

'Ladies and gentlemen,' she said, 'Now you are going to hear something which is not included on your programme. I have persuaded Miss Sylvia Weston, a gifted pupil of mine, to play for your pleasure some of Mr Chopin's compositions for the piano. Two Études, the first in E Flat and the second in C Minor, lastly his Polonaise.'

With her hand and a reassuring smile, she beckoned Sylvia to rise from her piano stool and come to the front of the stage. The girl did so, curtseyed diffidently to the politely applauding assembly and then, blushing prettily and profusely, returned to her seat. Laura withdrew to the wings.

Sylvia commenced playing and her playing was brilliant and spellbinding upon her listeners. At the conclusion of the Polonaise there was a moment of silence and then a torrent of clapping. Barnabas could see tears of pride in Thomas Weston's eyes as he too applauded his talented daughter. He reached out and gripped his friend's arm saying, 'She was good, Thomas, really good and now I think my Laura is pressing her to provide the encore being demanded!'

Laura, standing by the now risen Sylvia, signalled to Doctor Shillitoe indicating that he should use his gavel to command silence. When the noise had subsided she said, addressing the audience, 'I knew you would appreciate what you have just heard and now I am asking Miss Weston to play just one more piece. A nocturne, again by Mr Chopin.'

Sylvia seated herself and the lovely music, exquisitely played, flowed and held its listeners entranced. For a few moments time seemed to have stood still but when the last few notes had died away there followed an eruption of sound from those who had been listening, rising to their feet and giving the girl a standing ovation.

The concert was over. It had concluded with a mélange of national melodies for choir and orchestra arranged by Laura. 'Hearts of Oak' for England was followed by 'Over the Sea to Skye' for Scotland, 'Men of Harlech' for Wales and 'Danny Boy' for Ireland. In a grand finalé, with the audience joining in, 'Rule Britannia' was enthusiastically sung while a large Union Jack was unfurled and vigorously waved by Doctor Shillitoe standing on his table.

'A great success,' said Barnabas as arm in arm with Laura they made their brightly moonlit walk home together. 'A real triumph!'

'It was,' agreed Laura, 'Two hundred guineas raised for the infirmary and my protegé well and truly launched.'

'Your protegé? You mean, I suppose, Sylvia Weston?'

'Yes. Sylvia. Not that her launching means much, I'm afraid.'

'Why not, my dear? She is brilliant! Almost as good as you are, my love!'

Laura chuckled and squeezed his arm affectionately. 'As good as me?' she said, 'She's far better than I can ever be, Barnabas. She could be one of the world's greatest pianists given the right training. There's a man in Paris who could provide that but she won't consider going to him although her father is willing to meet all the expense involved.'

'Whyever not?'

'She's set her heart on something else!'

'What, my dear?'

'Getting married to the man she's just fallen head over heels in love with?'

'And who, pray is that?'

'Maurice Melton! If he hadn't arrived on the scene all would have been different. In two or three years she could be having audiences in the world's capitals at her feet but she is adamant. Paris and training, no! Maurice and marriage, yes!'

'He seems a nice enough young man.'

'He's nice enough, Barnabas, and he has all the attributes needed to make a good, kind and loving husband well able to look after a wife and children. Money is no problem. He comes of a wealthy family and he is well set on his own career with the bank. However it does mean that the concert platform will lose a great performer but then—' Laura paused before adding, 'then she's only doing what I would have chosen to do if I had been forced to make a choice between marrying you and a career. Thank goodness I wasn't and I've no regret, never a moment of it!'

Although at that moment they were passing under one of the few gaslamps in the road, Barnabas stopped, swept Laura up off her feet with his great arms and kissed her full on the lips. A following couple had to sidestep the laughing pair and the man, middle-aged and severe of face, muttered in passing, 'Disgraceful, Sir, disgraceful! You're both old enough to know better!'

'But how romantic!' murmured his wife enviously. 'How very romantic!'

# The Robbery Which Went Awry

It has been a gloomily overcast day with intermittent showers of rain and when darkness fell it seemed to fall both early and fast. With the coming of that darkness the rain poured down in earnest on the now almost deserted Hitchin Streets.

Three caped and cloth-capped horsemen rode through the puddles of Cock Street to its junction with Brand Street and came to a halt outside the London and County Bank. Two of the men dismounted and silently handed the reins of their horses to their still mounted companion. Then, having adjusted scarves to mask the lower part of their faces they drew weapons from their saddlebags and with these held at the ready, entered the bank. Their entry was not noticed by the three counter clerks and the three customers receiving attention until the raider carrying a sawn-off shotgun discharged one barrel at the ornate ceiling and noisily brought down a quantity of dust-raising plaster. Six pairs of eyes were then quickly focussed on the intruders.

One of the startled customers was an out of uniform Barnabas Tripp. He called out sharply, 'What the Hell does this mean?'

'It means,' came a muffled voice, 'that we're after money and you can take it, Mister, this pistol I'm pointing at your guts is likely to go off if you try stopping us. If you all do what we say and do it quick though, nobody is going to get hurt. You understand, don't you?'

The two farmers standing with Barnabas nodded their heads. So too did the bank clerks. Likewise also did Thomas Weston, the bank manager, who, on hearing the shot, had flung open his office door and now stood peering out of the doorway.

'Good! Then I want you all over there against that wall where I can see you!'

'There's my daughter with me in the office,' said Weston. 'Do you want her to come as well or can she stay in here?'

'No! Bring her out!'

Sylvia Weston, white faced and trembling followed her father from the office.

When the line had been formed to the raider's satisfaction he turned to his accomplice and said, pointing to the clerks, 'Take that bald-headed sod and make him fill your sack!' The second raider produced a sack from under his cape and handed this to the elderly man prodding him with the shotgun towards the heap of canvas bags neatly stacked by the doorway to the vault steps in readiness to be taken down for safekeeping overnight.

'Fill this,' he said sharply in a highly pitched and nervous voice. 'Red bags first and be quick!'

There was a sudden gasp from Sylvia on hearing this and she stared closely at the speaker. He, seeing her staring, made an attempt at raising his masking scarf a little higher. His eyes showed a flicker of fear but he continued in directing the bank clerk to the heap of bags and in supervising the filling of the sack. When he considered it contained as much weight as could be carried by the man he indicated it should be taken to the outer door of the bank.

'You won't get away with this,' said Barnabas to the raider with the pistol.

'We shall!' replied the man as his accomplice and the laden bank clerk disappeared into the street. 'We shall! We are getting away with it, Mister, real nice an' easy we are!'

There was an interrupting shout of 'You aren't you know! You aren't and you can drop that gun! Drop it!' The command had come from the bank manager's office doorway. Standing there, large revolver in hand, was Maurice Melton. The assistant manager had remained hidden in the office waiting for an opportunity to intervene to present itself. Then, with one raider out of the way, he had shown himself at the door with the weapon he had taken from the manager's desk.

His triumph was shortlived. The remaining bank robber responded immediately, not by dropping his gun but by firing it at Melton. Melton, with a surprised look on his face, swayed for a moment and then, with a bubble of blood from his mouth, fell forward first to his knees and them, countenance down, to the floor. The revolver was still in his hand.

Sylvia Weston screamed before collapsing in a fainting fit. Barnabas shouted, 'You'll hang for that, you bastard! That's murder!'

The killer laughed. He called out, 'And if anybody else tries anything I'll shoot again! So stay where you are,' and then backed to the open door to disappear quickly into the dimly lit street beyond. Within seconds those remaining in the bank heard the sharp clattering of horses' hooves fading away in the distance.


## Aftermath

'So we've precious little to go on,' said Sergeant Pearson following the account Barnabas had just given him of the late afternoon's events.

'Precious little indeed! We now know from the clerk who was made to carry out the money and fill the saddlebags that a third man was involved but like the other two raiders his face was hidden.

'And when last seen they were making for the London road?'

'They were and by now, if they pressed their horses they are more than halfway to their probably goal.'

'Tomorrow, Sir, we could make enquiries along the road. Maybe they even changed horses somewhere and we could get some descriptions of the bastards.'

'Perhaps, but I'm not too hopeful. The raid was well planned and their getaway, I expect, was equally well prepared. To my mind someone at local level is involved. They seemed to know when and where to go for the money and which bags they should take those which were best left. It was gold and paper money they were after and it was gold and paper money they got.'

'Do we know how much was stolen, Sir?'

'We know exactly how much. Sixteen hundred and forty-one pounds and ten shillings. All untraceable.'

'A fair haul, Sir?'

'A very fair haul as you say, Sergeant. Many other murders have been done for far less!'

Across the other side of Hitchin at nine o'clock that evening Silas Snode, DIck Bonsey and a very fearful and distressed looking Paul Weston were gathered around the table in the loft above the livery stable. The stolen money had been arranged in neat piles on the table. Snode, with a stub of pencil in his fingers, looked up from the scrap of paper on which he had been writing to say, 'Just over sixteen hundred and forty pounds. That's five hundred and fifty for me, five hundred and fifty for you, Dick, and the rest for you, Sonny Boy. Agreed?'

Bonsey agreed, 'Fair enough,' he said, 'but it don't seem much for a hanging job, does it?'

'Why did you shoot him,' asked Paul Weston in a tremulous voice. 'Why? Why? Why?"

'Why, you young fool, why? Because it was him dead or us getting nabbed and I wasn't having that. So that's why, boy, that's why. Now we've got clean away with it nobody's going to get caught, are they?'

Paul said, 'I hope not.'

'Hope not? What do you mean, hope not? You haven't done anything stupid, have your?'

'That girl—'

'The girl at the bank? What about her?'

'She's my sister. I think she recognised me!'

'Bloody Hell! That's why you've been half shitting yourself, is it?'

Snode, with his face contorted with rage, rose and went to a cupboard to turn from it, revolver in hand, and shot Weston neatly between the eyes. As his body slumped forward across the table it scattered many of the piles of coins, some of which fell to the floor.

'God!' exclaimed the appalled Bonsey. 'What the devil have you done now? What the devil made you do that?'

'What have I done? I've silenced the little sod once and for all – for bloody all! If his sister blabs and tells the police they'll soon be looking for him and we can't take the chance that he wouldn't talk if they caught him. And if he had talked then the buggering police would soon be after us. No! It's best he's dead! It also means me and you have more to share, don't it, Dick buddy?'

'But what can we do with his body? It can't stay here!'

'It can't and it won't. I know exactly where we can dump it. Somewhere it won't be found in a hurry, maybe never!'

'Where, Silas, where?'

Snode told him and Bonsey grinned. 'Under the bluebells, eh!'

'Yes, under the lovely bluebells!'

A much distressed Sylvia Weston did tell her father that evening that she was sure one fo the bank robbers had been her brother.

'That's impossible,' said the astonished Thomas Weston. 'Absolutely impossible. Paul would never get himself mixed up with thieves and murderers. He's a good boy, a little wild at times perhaps but he's no criminal. Of that I am sure. I know I wasn't as close to that second wretch as you were, my dear, but I'm certain it wasn't Paul. It just couldn't have been. I know you are terribly upset by what has happened to Maurice today but you are quite wrong about Paul. Quite wrong!'

Mention of Maurice Melton's name had brought a fresh sobbing outburst of tears from his daughter and Weston called for his housekeeper, a gentle kindly woman, to help get the girl to her bed making sure that she took the sleeping potion which Doctor Shillitoe had left for her.

After Sylvia had retired, the banker resolved that come what may he would, on the following day, take steps to prove beyond doubt that Paul had not been involved in the robbery and the tragic death of Melton.

# A Book of Revelations

Late in the afternoon of the next day a much agitated Thomas Weston called at Hitchin police station and was immediately shown through to the inner office where Barnabas was seated alone at his desk.

'What is it, Thomas?' enquired the inspector seeing his friend's troubled face. 'What has happened now to give you further distress?'

'It's Paul, that son of mine,' replied the banker. 'He seems to have disappeared!'

'Disappeared? What do you mean, disappeared?'

'He's gone! Fled, I fear!' Tears were now running down Weston's cheeks as Barnabas quickly rose to close the office door.

'Fled? Fled from what, Thomas?'

'Of that I'm not certain but I am afraid it is something really dreadful.' Weston hesitated and then went on, 'Last evening Sylvia told me she was certain one of the men involved in the robbery and the murder of Melton was her brother Paul. She'd recognised him despite the masking scarf and she thinks he knew she had done so. I told her that she must be mistaken and packed her off to bed but thinking about it after she had gone up to her room brought some doubts to my mind. She had been so sure she was right. So very, very sure!'

'So?'

'So I decided I would go to Cambridge this morning and confront the boy at his lodgings.'

'But he wasn't there?'

'No, he wasn't. His landlady said he had gone off early yesterday and had not returned although he had said he would be back in the evening and be able to settle up with her.'

'Settle up with her?'

'Yes. Apparently he owes quite a lot of rent for his room but then, as she said, he seemed to owe several people money. One in particular, a bookmaker, had called at the house and she had heard him threatening Paul. Shouting he was!'

'That doesn't sound very good.'

'It didn't sound good to me. I asked to see his room and she showed me up to it. I had a quick look round. All his spare clothes seemed to be there so he must have intended coming back. I found a number of unpaid bills in a drawer and I also found this.'

Weston handed Barnabas a small black notebook. The inspector opened it and carefully examined some of the pages. 'It seems to be some kind of diary,' he said looking up at the banker.

'It is a kind of diary, I agree, Barnabas. It records his winnings and his losings at the races, cockfighting and cards. There is also mention of payments to someone named Freda.'

'Yes and I see in one place that he refers to her as a bloodsucking little bitch. But what interests me most are notes concerning visits to Hitchin. I thought you said that you hadn't seen much of him of late?'

'I did tell you that. We've scarce seen him since vacation time when I had him for a while at the bank to gain experience.'

Barnabas again fingered through some of the pages. 'Well,' he said, 'he does seem to have visited Hitchin several times recently and met up with a "B" and an "S" at "D" wherever that may be. Do the letters mean anything to you, Thomas?'

'No, Barnabas, they don't. They mean nothing.'

'And they mean nothing to me at the moment but we can make some enquiries. I certainly don't like the look of things I'm sorry to say and I can offer you nothing for your comfort, Thomas. I can only suggest that we wait for developments. there are bound to be some and let us hope they will lead to clearing you son's name and that, in the end, he will turn up safe and sound.'

# Developments

It was midmorning of the following day, Friday, when Tommy, the son of Kit Elder, the St. Ippollitts woman poacher, called on Barnabas with a message from his mother. 'She says,' he said, 'you'd best come with me right away with two of your men and a couple of shovels.'

'Come where and what for, Tommy?'

'Our place first. She'll be waiting for us there and as for what for I guess it's to dig up a body 'cos she also said you'd best bring a coffin with you!'

'Whose body?'

'Don't know and I don't think she knows either. You can use my cart if you like. I've delivered all the eggs and chickens I had to deliver in Hitchin today. Delivered 'em all.'

So it was within a very short time Barnabas, Sergeant Pearson and two constables rode out of the police station yard followed by Tommy and his horse and cart. The shovels, together with a deal coffin borrowed from Mr Jepps, the undertaker, were on the cart concealed by a tarpaulin and the small procession attracted little attention as it passed along Bancroft and through the town.

At Little Almshoe Barnabas dismounted and entered the kitchen of the poacher's cottage to find Kit busy cleaning and oiling her gun. She greeted him like the old friend that he had become over the years, with a smile on her brown, weatherbeaten face saying, 'I shan't keep you a moment, Mr Barnabas, just a last rub over afore I puts her away. I never does leave my Betsy dirty. It don't do and she wouldn't like it, would she?'

'I don't suppose she would,' replied Barnabas with a grin. 'Served you well again last night did she?'

Kit chuckled as she gave the wooden stock of her gun a final fond polish with her apron before securing it on two hooks in the chimney breast. 'Last night? Now what would I be doing out at night with a gun? I ask you, what?'

'What indeed, Kit? Listening to the nightingales perhaps?'

'Yes, Mr Barnabas. In a wood they were.'

'Which wood?'

'Hitch Wood.'

'Now tell me what happened in Hitch Wood.'

'I came across something being buried.'

'Interesting! Tell me more.'

'It wasn't all that far from the road. I saw a lantern burning and I crept up curious like to get a good look at things.'

'And what was happening?'

'Two men with shovels were digging a hole. A third man lay stretched out on the ground who didn't move. He was dead I reckon.'

'You watched them bury the body?'

'I did. I just watched and saw them fill in the grave and cover it with leaves.'

'Then?'

'When they'd finished I followed them.'

'Where to?'

'The edge of the wood and the road where there was a trap and pony waiting.

'And you saw them drive off?'

'I did. Laughing they were. Laughing softlike and talking excited like, though I couldn't hear what they was saying.'

'Do you know who they were or can you give me any description of them?

Kit Elder shook her head and said, 'The lantern didn't give that much light and I didn't get all that close to them. One did speak with a voice which wasn't local like and I reckon I might know him if I heard him speak again.'

With this Barnabas had to be satisfied for the moment and then, with Kit sitting by her son's side on the cart, the small procession set off for Hitch Wood.

They had no difficulty in locating the shallow grave but were horrified to see when the body was uncovered that the face of the dead man had been mutilated so badly, probably by a shovel, he was quite unrecognisable.

'He weren't no age, Sir,' volunteered Sergeant Pearson. 'No more than about twenty, I'd say.'

'Which makes me fairly certain it's the missing Paul Weston,' said Barnabas, 'and I'm not looking forward to getting his father to identify him, I'm really not.'

Later than day when the bank manager was called into the infirmary mortuary to view the body, he, with tears in his eyes quickly resolved the problem. 'There's a birthmark on my boy's left buttock shaped like a pear,' he said and the mortuary attendant nodded and muttered, 'Yes, there's a mark on 'im, there is. I saw it when I took off 'is britches. Pear shaped, about the size of me 'and it is.'

'And how did he die?' asked Weston. 'Tell me Barnabas, tell me.'

'He died quickly, Thomas, very quickly. A bullet in the brain, so Doctor Shillitoe says and death was instantaneous.'

'Thank God he didn't suffer but why did he have to die, Barnabas, why?'

'He knew too much, Thomas, he knew too much about the bank robbery and the killing of Maurice Melton, I'm afraid. He had to be silenced!'

'You'll get his murderers, Barnabas, won't you? You'll get them hanged?'

'Yes, we shall get them!' Barnabas assured him solemnly. 'We shall get them all right and I've no doubt they'll hang.'

'Good!' Thomas Weston took one last look at what again lay completely covered on the mortuary bench and turning, stiff-backed, made for the side door of the mortuary.


## At the Half Moon Tavern

Intensive enquiries by Barnabas, his sergeant and his constables had revealed only a little about the movements of Paul Weston on the day of the bank raid which, according to Doctor Shillitoe, was also the most likely day of his death.

Barnabas, seated at his desk, regarded the photograph before him with a puzzled frown. It was a portrait of the young man taken earlier in the year by the town's photographer, Thomas Latchmore, and one of the several prints he had supplied to help the police with their enquiries. Tapping it with his finger he looked across to where Sergeant Pearson stood in the doorway and asked, 'You showed your copy to Tilly Jones and she was absolutely certain that it was Weston who called on her that morning?'

'Yes, Sir, absolutely certain. He came to her just before noon.'

'That's early for a call on a prostitute, isn't it?'

'Early but eager, Sir. He's been early on previous occasions. She reckons he'd come straight off the Cambridge train and was desperate for a woman. He was all excited like this time she said and shot his lot the moment she touched him!'

'Did he, indeed? But he didn't leave her immediately?'

'No. She said she calmed him down and later he managed things better. When he did leave her about two o'clock he didn't give her the two pounds she'd asked for but gave her three and went of cock-a-hoop!'

'Cock-a-hoop? Well I suppose that's one way of putting it but did she know where he was going?'

'She says he murmured something about having to meet a man at the Half Moon.'

'The tavern at Bull Corner? Seedy sort of place these days, isn't it?'

'Yes, Sir. Run down, Sir, since that American, Snode, took over.'

'You made enquiries there?'

'I did. I saw Snode and showed him the picture but he said he'd never seen Weston and he didn't have gents like him as customers.'

'Snode, you say?'

'Yes, Snode, Sir. Silas Snode.'

'American, you said?'

'I did. He's been over here for a few years but still has that drawly way of speaking.'

'Does he now? I wonder. I wonder!'

Barnabas opened Paul Weston's little black book and referred to an entry therein saying, 'He writes about meeting up with a "B" and an "S" at "D". Supposing, just supposing, "S" is Snode and the "D" is not a letter but a half moon. Who then is "B"?'

'The livery stable in the Half Moon yard is owned by a man named Bonsey. I do know that, Sir.'

'A livery stable? Horses? A man named Bonsey. "B" represents Bonsey?'

'It ties up, Sir.' Pearson sounded excited and eager. 'It all ties up! Weston has been meeting up with Snode and Bonsey at the Half Moon and Bonsey provided the horses for the raid on the bank!'

'And you can hold your horses, Sergeant. We shall need more than these notes in a diary and our surmises to pin anything on Snode and Bonsey.'

'We could question them Sir, and search their premises. We've surely enough on them to get a warrant for a search, haven't we?'

'Only about enough. I shall have a word with Squire Radcliffe. He is the most likely magistrate to sign one for us.'

'And if he does, what then, Sir?'

'We shall take four men, question Snode and Bonsey and make a very thorough search.'

'Do we go armed?'

'Yes! Armed. The constables will carry rifles, we will carry pistols. If they are the men we are looking for they are highly dangerous. They've already killed twice. We must take no chances, Sergeant, no chances at all!'

With a warrant duly signed by Mr Delme Radcliffe the small, grim-faced posse set off at three o'clock from the police station causing many heads to turn as it marched briskly along the busy Bancroft and Cock Street and then on through the market

square and Sun Street. At the top of Bridge Street it halted at
Bull Corner and the constables, at the double, were posted with
rifles loaded at the ready, to guard the exits from the Half
Moon tavern and the tavern yard.

Barnabas and Sergeant Pearson then entered the tavern,
pistols in hand, to find the taproom deserted. Barnabas, with an
empty pewter tankard, rapped heavily on the bar counter until
a woman appeared at an inner door. She seemed dazed, both
eyes were blackened and half closed. Her lips were swollen,
split and bleeding and it was obvious that she had only just
been badly beaten up.

'Mistress Snode?' Barnabas asked gently.

The woman nodded.

'Who has done this to you? Your husband?'

Again the woman nodded.

'The wretch! Why did he do that?'

'Why? He caught me taking money from a bag I found
hidden in the outhouse.'

'What sort of bag?' queries Pearson.

'A red bag! It was full of gold coins and he knows I
need money badly. He went mad and hit me! He kept on
hitting me!'

Pearson gave Barnabas a significant look and then asked the
woman, 'Where is your husband now?'

'He's gone across the yard to me brother's place.'

'The livery stable? Bonsey's Livery Stable?'

'Yes. The two of them are as thick as thieves, they are. Dick
won't do anything to help me, he won't. I know he won't!'

'He won't, woman! He sure won't!'

The rough voice came loud and strong from behind Mrs
Snode as an arm reached round her neck and the man who had
shouted, shielded by her body, clapped a pistol to her head.
'Make one move, either of you, and she gets it. Then I shall
shoot you! Both of you!'

'You won't get away with this, Snode,' said Barnabas calmly.
There are men outside and they are all armed!'

Snode laughed. 'I know. I spotted them when they took up

their positions. Hicks they are, country hicks! Never fired at anybody in their lives! Any of them! And as for you, woman—' Snode's eyes were on the policemen but his words were directed at his wife '– as for you, you silly bitch, you've been saying things that could get me and Dick hung, you have!'

'And hang you will!' said Barnabas firmly.

'But hang we shan't,' replied Snode. 'You won't catch us! Dick's saddling up a couple of his best horses and there's a backway out of the yard to a lane which you haven't got covered. We'll be miles out of our way before you can get mounts to follow us!'

'Think so?' said Pearson sharply as he fired his pistol from the hip. The bullet grazed Snode's right elbow with numbing effect on his forearm and hand and he dropped his gun. Quick thinking, however, he flung down his wife to the floor, pushed her to one side with his foot and slammed the door between himself and the policemen.

'Damn!' exclaimed Barnabas.

'Now what, Sir? What about her? She seems to be in some sort of faint.'

'Leave her, Sergeant, leave her. We must get into the yard and stop the pair of them getting away. Quick now and keep your gun at the ready. Snode's lost his but Bonsey may have a shooter!'

'He probably has, Sir, he probably has!'


## Conflagration

With Sergeant Pearson following closely behind him Barnabas cautiously emerged from the kitchen doorway and stepped into the cobbled yard shared by the tavern and the livery stable. Then, when scarcely outside, both men crouched down instinctively as a sharp fusillade of shots from the constables under the arched gateway sent bullets whistling over their heads. The bullets were an effective warning to Snode and

Bonsey who were attempting to approach the pair of saddled horses tethered further up the yard and the two men ran back into the barn from which they had come.

Barnabas and Pearson stood up. 'Now we've got 'em cornered!' said the sergeant. 'Properly cornered we have!'

'Cornered and dangerous and we don't want any casualties, do we?'

'That we don't!' Pearson sounded emphatic. 'We certainly don't!'

At that moment a small, white-whiskered, old man peered nervously round the door of the barn into which Snode and Bonsey had disappeared. His hands were held high and he cried out, 'Don't shoot, Mister! Don't shoot!' as he ran across the yard to join the inspector and the sergeant. 'Don't shoot!'

'And you, old fellow,' asked Barnabas as the trembling man stood before him, 'who are you? And you can put your hands down for a start!'

'Me? Me name's Green, Sir, Dozer Green they calls me, an' I do odd jobs round the yard for Mr Snode and Mr Bonsey, I do. An' I'm proper strong I am though I do be seventy-five. They don't pay me much but 'er at the Moon, she gives me an 'ot dinner most days. She's all right, she is. I likes 'er, I does.' Having said this, Dozer lowered his hands to continue with 'That shootin', that frit me that did. Proper frit me!'

'Frightened you did it, Dozer? Well it was meant to frighten Snode and Bonsey from going off on their horses. We intend to arrest them. Arrest them for murder!'

'I ain't surprised, Mister. Them's a bad lot they are, specially that Snode. I 'eard 'im tell once 'ow 'e shot a man in Mericky an' got away with it.'

'Well, he's not going to get away with it here now we've got the pair of them trapped in that barn. What's in the barn and why were you in there?'

'Straw an' 'ay and a loft place where Bonsey lives.'

'There's no other way out?'

'Not that I knows of, Mister, an' I was in there 'anging the lighted lantern I puts at the bottom of the stairs every afternoon just afore it gets proper dark.'

Barnabas looked at Pearson and the sergeant grinned before saying, 'If there is no other way out then we haven't got much to worry about, have we. They'll have to come out of that doorway sooner or later and all we've got to do is wait and watch it. By my reckoning they won't try to break out before it is properly dark and that won't be all that long.'

Looking out from the dirty dormer window in the loft roof Snode and Bonsey had only a very limited view of the yard but Bonsey had been Dozer Green talking to the policemen and afterwards scuttle along the yard to enter the kitchen doorway.

Snode, despite the considerable pain in his injured elbow chuckled. He said, 'I guess the old fool will have told them there ain't no way out of here except by the doorway and we'd sure be fools if we tried that, wouldn't we?'

'We sure would!' Bonsey was looking up at the skylight in the side of the barn roof hidden from the Half Moon's yard. 'That should be dead easy. Out through there, down over Deacon's bakery and into his yard and those bloody policemen won't see a thing!'

'And once we're in Back Street we aim for the Black Lion. George Tipping will give us shelter there until the heat is off. Then we make for London.'

'You're sure of George?'

'If we pay him enough.'

'Can we? Most of the money is with the horses.'

'We've enough in our belts and George isn't a greedy bugger. He himself has good reasons for not liking the police and he won't see us hang!'

Then, much to Bonsey's surprise Snode picked up one of the two pistols on the table using his left hand and said, 'I'm not quite so good with this but good enough.'

'For what? Good enough for what, Silas?'

'To put out the bloody lamp at the bottom of the stairs!'

'Why? We're not going out that way!'

'No. But I want them to think we are!'

'Be careful!'

'I shall! Now open the trap for me.'

Bonsey did as asked and Snode began to descend the top steps into the lower part of the barn. When he got a clear view of the lantern he fired one shot to shatter the glass. The shot did more than that. Blobs of burning oil were splattered in all directions, some over the piled hay and straw. In a moment the gobbets of light joined up in a great wall of flame. Snode, cursing, hastily retreated back up the steps and Bonsey slammed the trapdoor on the inferno already raging below.

'Out!' shouted Snode. 'Out! Out now! We can't stay here! Out! Out now!'

Bonsey gawped at him open mouthed. Fear showing in his eyes. 'What? What?' he croaked eventually. 'What?'

'Out! Bloody out! Bloody quick! Put that bloody chair on the table and get up to the skylight! We're going out now!'

Doing as bidden, Bonsey placed the chair on the table and climbed up to stand on its seat. His first push on the small skylight failed to open it. A second and more vigorous attempt also failed and he looked down at Snode with panic plain upon his face.

'Push again!' shouted Snode holding aloft the lit candle which had been standing in a saucer on the table. 'Push again, you silly bugger! Push again! It must go!'

'It won't!'

'Why not?'

'It's been nailed fast! Nailed! Nailed!'

Smoke was already beginning to billow up through the gaps between the rough floor boards. Bonsey, who had clambered down to crouch near Snode, began to whimper. The whimper developed into a scream as the first flames began licking at his ankles. Snode put his pistol into the open mouth, shot him, and then, with a curious smile on his face, shot himself.

It took until dawn for the hastily summoned fire brigade to bring the flames under control and most of the yard buildings

had been gutted by the spreading blaze. At midday two badly
charred bodies were recovered from the ruined haybarn and
laid out on the wet cobbles to be covered by a sheet of green
canvas. Barnabas and Sergeant Pearson, having been sent for to
view the remains, did so with satisfaction.

Pearson said, 'Best thing that could have happened, Sir. It
has saved a trial and a couple of hangings and we've got back
most of the money they stole from the bank. Even what must
have been in their money belts!'

'Yes, but it's been a very nasty business, Sergeant. Two
young lives lost, a father bereaved and a girl heartbroken. No
good has come out of it. None at all.'

But Barnabas was not entirely right. Six months later when,
at Mrs Snode's pressing invitation, he and Sergeant Pearson
called at the Half Moon, they found it a bright, clean, cheerful
place with many customers and a smartly dressed, smiling
landlady to greet them.

'Are you on or off duty, Inspector?' she asked.

'Off duty! Both of us, Madam.'

'Then you must have a drink on the house. Strong ale? Or
spirits, perhaps?'

'Strong ale,' replied Barnabas after a quick look at Pearson.
'You seem to be doing well, Mrs Snode, very well?'

'Very well, aren't we Dozer? she replied appealing to the
now apron clad little man who was helping her behind the bar.

'Aye! We are an' all. Gettin' along fine, we are. Me, special
like now there ain't much yard work an' I'm in 'ere reg'lar with
no 'osses ter look after. I 'ates 'osses!'

'You've finished with the livery stable them, Mrs Snode?'

'Yes, I have, Inspector, I have. I've used the insurance money
I got for the buildings to get this place on its feet again and
we're doing quite nicely, thank you!'

'You've done well, Madam, very well!'

That evening, over their bedtime cocoa, Barnabas told Laura
about the transformation of the Half Moon tavern and with a
twitch of amusement on her lips she gave him the good news of
the day.

'Sylvia Weston,' she commenced.

'What about Sylvia?'

'She's going to Paris. Going to the teacher I suggested.'

'So you are pleased?'

'Very! She is now going to be one of the world's finest pianists. I am sure of that, really sure!'

'But her father? Won't he be lonely left on his own?'

Laura chortled rather wickedly. 'He won't be on his own,' she said. 'He's getting married again.'

'What? Who?'

'That rather prim young housekeeper of his. He's put her in the family way!'

Barnabas laughed loud and long and then said, wiping the tears of merriment from his eyes, 'The sly old dog! I didn't think he had it in him!'

There was a sly smile from Laura. 'There's a comment,' she said 'with which I could cap that, my love, but being a lady and properly brought up, I shall refrain from doing so!'

# THE CASE OF THE
# BLACKSMITH'S REVENGE

## The Blacksmith's Daughter

Barnabas was initiated into the craft of Freemasonry soon after his promotion to the rank of inspector. At the ceremony, after first enduring in darkness the perils of a sharp poniard held firmly at his naked left breast and a running noose constricting his neck, his blindfold had eventually been removed, allowing him to look up into the smiling eyes of the Worshipful Master of the Lodge. And that year that Worshipful Master of Hitchin's Wilshere Lodge had been George Barker, the blacksmith, whose forge and large cottage home were situated in the great yard behind the Swan Inn on the west side of the market square.

The two men had become firm friends both in and out of the Lodge and Barnabas became a frequent caller at the smithy where the golden bearded George and his two strapping sons not only shod horses but skilfully produced, among other things, ornate wrought iron gates, delicate screens and decorative grills of the highest artistic quality.

One fine morning, but a cold one, early in December Barnabas had occasion to call at the forge with a pair of handcuffs requiring a smith's attention, but while passing under the archway into the inn yard found himself being forced to press back against the wall by three young and noisy horsemen riding past him abreast who seemed to ignore his presence completely.

'Young pups!' he muttered aloud as he emerged into the yard and passed by the open doorway to the workshop in which stood Amos Day, the basket maker, partly woven basket in hand, who had witnessed the inspector's discomfiture.

'Aye, Sir,' he called out. 'Aye, Sir, I agree, Proper young pups them three be, Sir. Think they can do just as they please, just 'cos their fathers own bits of land hereabouts and they sits on the local Bench. Need talkin' to them does. You could 'ave been 'urt you could!'

'I could have been but I wasn't, Amos. Next Tuesday when I expect to see their fathers at Court I will have a word with them and get them to discipline their sons. They've been nothing but troublemakers since the college vacations began and they've been home from Cambridge. They need checking before they get themselves involved in something really nasty.'

'Aye! You do that, Sir. You get their fathers 'aving a go at 'em! I should, if I were you, Sir!'

Barnabas, still fuming, proceeded up the yard until he reached the forge, where outside, tethered to a rail were two horses waiting to be reshod. Over the doorway a newly painted sign read 'George Barker & Sons – Shoeing & General Smiths'.

George Barker, leather aproned and in his shirt sleeves, came forward to greet the policeman and nodding in the direction of his sign asked, 'Like it, Barnabas?'

'Very smart, old friend. So you've now taken in the twins as partners?'

'I have, indeed. I have. They're of age now and out of their 'prenticeship time. Both of them are good smiths and I couldn't ask for better. That I couldn't!'

'I'm glad to hear it! You've a right to be proud of them and I'm sure they'll do well for you and themselves. They're not like the trash who are just stabling their horses at the top end of the yard.'

George Barker slowly shook his head as he turned to view the trio. 'Them!' Disgust showed in his face. 'I saw 'em ride past, damn them! They've taken to stabling their nags here these last few days when they've been coming into the town, mischief bound. I'm sorry now the coaches are finished, that the stabling still stands and is let out for next to nothing to any Tom, Dick or Harry, who wants it for the day.'

'Have they been giving you any special bother?'

'No Barnabas, they haven't but I don't like the way they behave when our Sally is about. Lots of silly remarks they make. Some of them not nice for a young woman to hear and put up with when they pass her by.'

'Your Sally? She's eighteen now I suppose?'

'Eighteen she is and just like her mother was at eighteen and I courted her. Pretty as a picture. If she were alive she'd be as proud of her as I am of my boys. She's a right good cook too, is our Sal and looks after me and her brothers just like her mother would have done. Dear Annie!'

'You still grieve for her, George?'

'Aye, Barnabas. Almost two years gone and I still miss her badly, I reckon I always shall, though I've much to be thankful for in the family I've still got left.'

George led Barnabas not into the forge where the furnace was roaring and the twins were hammering noisily at their anvils, but took him into the adjoining cottage where, after seating his visitor down in the kitchen, he poured out two tankards of ale and set these on the well scrubbed table.

'No Sally about?' enquired Barnabas.

'Gone for a dozen eggs. She gets them from Widow Hilton who keeps a few hens at the back of her cottage in Nuns Close.'

'I know her, George. She's the mother of Arthur Hilton, one of my constables. Good man, Arthur, very steady.'

'Yes, I agree. I reckon he's got an eye on our Sally, has young Arthur, and I've also a feeling she's got an eye on him.'

'Do you approve?'

'I'm not interfering. No, I shan't interfere.' The blacksmith supped at his ale and then said, 'I suppose you've brought those cuffs you told me about at last meeting?'

'I have.'

Barnabas produced the handcuffs from his pocket and gave these over to George for inspection. They were examined with care and pronounced upon as being worth repairing.

'It will only take about twenty minutes to put right and I'll get them done now if you're prepared to wait.'

'Twenty minutes? I am. I've nothing pressing at the moment.'

'Then I'll give them to one of the boys and then come back to you. There's a favour I want to ask.'

'Ask it. If I can grant it I most certainly will. It's not a police matter, I take it?'

George laughed. 'No brother, Masonic, I'm in no trouble with the law. Not that I know about.'

On his return to the kitchen the smith said, 'I want to put both boys up for the Lodge. Watchmaker Street is willing to propose them. Will you second the proposals?'

'Willingly! Most willingly!'

'Thank you. I was sure you would be and now I can have a word with Brother Secretary and get things moving.'

'Yes, George, you can. They'll be taking a step they'll never regret as you know, and I know. Who is the elder of the pair? Sebastian or David?'

'Seb, by twenty-five mintues.'

'So he'll take precedence?'

'He will—'

Before any more could be said the door was violently pushed open and an obviously much distressed young woman rushed in to put the basked she was carrying on the table before bursting into tears.

'What's happened, Sal?' asked her father rising to take her in his arms to comfort her. 'What's happened, my dear?'

'Those men!' she sobbed. 'Those awful men!'

'What men?' asked the smith.

'Them at the stable. Specially the one they called Clarry!'

'Young Clarence Harding,' put in Barnabas. 'Son of Sir Oliver of Pirton Court! He was among the three that passed me.'

'And what did he do?' queried George Barker angrily.

'He pushed me against the door of the stable and—'

'And what?'

'He tried to kiss me and put his hand up my skirt but I marked him and got away!'

'Marked him, girl? How did you mark him?'

'I ran my nails down his cheek, I did, father. Ran them real hard and deep!'

'Good for you!' said Barnabas rising from his seat, 'but that's not enough. I want a word with that young scoundrel. A sharp word!'

'So do I,' said the blacksmith fiercely, 'and I'll mark him as well!'

But when Barnabas and George Barker reached the stable the three youths and their horses were gone. The dull witted boy, Timmy Ward, who for coppers tended to the horses left at the stable, emerged from one of the stalls to say, when questioned 'Gone out the back way they 'ave. Went off proper quick like. Din't pay me nothin' neither they din't. Nothin'!'

Barnabas gave the boy a coin and then asked 'Did you hear them say which way they were going, Timmy?'

Timmy shook his head and George Barker said, 'You won't get much sense out of him, Barnabas, he's short of tuppence in the shilling at the best of times!'

'No, I ain't,' Timmy sounded indignant. 'I'm all there all right an' don't 'e say diff'rent Mr Barker. Don't 'e say diff'rent. I ain't tuppence short of nothin', I aren't!'

Two of the three horsemen trotting along the road from Hitchin to Pirton village occasionally chuckled with laughter at the third rider who from time to time pressed a bloodied handkerchief to his left cheek.

'Sodding little hellcat,' he complained bitterly. 'You two silly buggers can laugh if you like! I can't! She's spoiled me looks, she has!'

'You asked for it, Clarry, trying to grope her,' said the redheaded Greenway unsympathetically. 'You got it good and proper, you did!'

'Yes,' agreed the third rider, Jabez Nelson. 'You got it real good and real proper. Serves you right!'

'I'll do her for it!' muttered Harding. 'Yes, I'll do her all right! I'll make her pay for it! You'll see! Bloody little bitch! She'll pay!'

'How?' queried Nelson, grinning. 'How will you make her pay for it, Clarry?'

'I'll put my seven inches right between her legs I will and see how she likes that!'

'What? Take her by force?' Greenway seemed shocked. 'Don't be a fool, Clarry, don't be a fool. You could get into real trouble if you tried anything like that. Forget it, man, forget it!'

'Yes!' agreed Nelson. 'You'd far better forget and leave the girl alone.'

'Shan't!' said Harding emphatically. 'I'll get a leg across her if it's the last thing I ever do. I swear I will!'

'Well don't count us in on something that stupid,' said Nelson, to which Greenway added, 'Not bloody likely! We ain't that mad!'

'Then to hell with you both!' shouted Harding kicking his spurs viciously into his horse's flanks and galloping off ahead of his two companions.

## The Raping of Sally Barker

It was two days later when Clarence Harding wreaked his revenge on Sally Barker. The rape was violent and viciously carried out at knifepoint in one of the horse boxes in the Swan Inn yard. It was witnessed by a gawping Timmy Ward who was much too terrified to help the girl.

It occurred just before noon, and just as St. Mary's church clock was striking the hour of twelve the screaming Sally ran into the forge and poured out her account of the outrage to her appalled father and brothers.

They, scarcely waiting for her to finish what she was saying, rushed up to the stables only to find their quarry had fled, with the trembling Timmy not even able to say or indicate the direction taken by Harding.

Barnabas, having been quickly informed by George Barker of what had happened, soon had his constables looking for the

youth and Harding was found, late in the afternoon, dazed
with brandy drinking, in the tap room of the Black Lion public
house in Back Street. The finder was Constable Hilton, and
Harding was not handled gently as with some difficulty he was
dragged to the police station to be thrown into a cell to sober up.

'We'd better get word of this to his father, hadn't we, Sir?'
queried Sergeant Pearson as he and Barnabas stood at the open
cell door looking down at the crumpled figure on the
straw-strewn floor.

'And right proud of his son and heir will Sir Oliver be if he
arrives to find him in this state,' replied Barnabas, stirring the
baronet's son with a none too gentle boot. He went on with,
'Seven girls he had to sire before he fathered this monstrosity to
inherit the title and the Pirton acres. Seven girls and in the end
this shit!'

'Aye, Sir, shit Sir, proper shit, Sir! And there's been many a
laugh hereabouts regarding that. Sir Bloody Oliver could make
teapots all right but he couldn't put spouts on 'em until this bit
of nastiness turned up.'

'Perhaps a spell in prison will do him some good,' observed
Barnabas.

'Five years hard! That's what he deserves,' said Pearson,
closing and locking the cell door. 'Five years hard!'

But Clarence Harding never went to prison. When the case was
brought to the local Bench the magistrates, two of whom were
close friends of the father, dismissed the charge and a grinning
Harding went free. A clever London lawyer had represented
him and twisted Timmy Ward's evidence into the suggestion
that Sally Barker had enticed Harding into the stable and had
even been a willing participant in what had followed.

'Somebody must have got at Timmy,' said Sergeant Pearson
as he and a disgusted Barnabas left the courtroom. 'I'm sure of
it! Damn sure!'

'Being sure of it and being able to prove there has been

bribery are two different matter,' replied Barnabas, 'but it is more than likely that for a couple of sovereigns Timmy would say whatever he was told to say and even believe he was telling the truth when he was saying it!'

'Aye, Sir, I agree. I reckon you may be right.'

But Barnabas was not quite right in his assumption. The clerk of the clever lawyer had pressed five, not two sovereigns into Timmy's receptive hand early in the morning of the day of the trial.

Over supper that evening when Barnabas told Laura of what had happened she said sadly, 'It's Sally I worry about, Barnabas. Not only has she been outraged by that wretch but her name has been blackened beyond belief by those court proceedings. Is there nothing you can do about it, my dear?'

'Not a thing, dearest, not a single thing. I'm afraid. But I wouldn't put it beyond George Barker and his sons doing something. I really wouldn't!'

## The Tragedy at West Mill

Barnabas liked fly fishing and was very good at it. On some afternoons when he was free from duty he would spend a happy hour or so on the banks of the River Oughton which ran through the pleasant meadowland to the north of Hitchin and abounded with trout.

On the damp, drizzly afternoon of the day following the Harding trial, having had some success with his casting on the more open stretches of the river – the two and a half pounder and the two pounder in his basket being proof of this – he decided to try his luck in the West Mill millpond in the hope that he could land one of the monster trout which lurked in that stretch of deeper water.

'One really big one,' he murmured to himself as he approached the pond, 'and I'll go home content.'

A flash of brilliant blue attracted his attention as a kingfisher made for a tree on the opposite bank the branches of which trailed in the fairly fast moving current. Then caught up in the bushes on the bank beneath him, there was something else which was blue in colour. It was a woman's cloak spreading out from a body which lay face downward in the water. Appalled, he stared down at this for a moment or two before putting down his fishing tackle and attempting to drag what was obviously a corpse on to the riverside footpath. Although he realised he could do nothing to help her he felt he must get her on the bank and turn her face uppermost. He managed the task with some difficulty, getting wet feet and wet legs in the process and having done what he had set out to achieve he drew to one side the long, luxuriant hair which concealed her features. There was instant recognition. The body was that of the unfortunate Sally Barker. Much distressed he set off for the mill to get assistance.

An hour later, after Sally's remains had been gently taken and laid in one of the miller's barns, the miller, Saul Burry, took Barnabas into Hitchin in his trap to break the sad news to the girl's father.

'A most unfortunate young woman,' Burry had said after Barnabas had told him what had led up to the girl's suicide. 'Most unfortunate but she had no need to do herself in like she has done, had she?'

'No,' agreed Barnabas, 'she hadn't, but what really galls me is that the wretched youth responsible for her dishonour and death is to pay no penalty for what he has done and I doubt when he does hear of what has now happened if he even feels any remorse.'

George Barker, the blacksmith, could say little when Barnabas broke the news to him but tears sprang to his eyes and after a moment or so he said chokingly, 'You'd best leave me and her brothers to our grief, Barnabas, but as God is my witness Clarence Harding is going to suffer for what he has done. Suffer! Really suffer! We shall see to that!'

Barnabas had shaken his head and cautioned his friend. 'Do nothing rash in your anger, George. Nothing to make matters worse than they are. Don't, I beg you, take the law into your own hands. No good will come of it. No good at all!'

But that evening the blacksmith took a stout kitchen knife from its rack and, with his two sons watching him, knowing what he had in mind, he began to sharpen its gleaming blade on a whetstone.

'When, father, when?' asked Sebastian.

'When, Seb? When?' There was a grim look on George Barker's countenance. 'At the first opportunity which presents itself, Seb, at the very first opportunity.'

'And afterwards? queried David.

'Afterwards, Dave? Afterwards we get out from here to foreign parts. I've a fancy for a faraway place where different stars look down at night and the air smells fresher and cleaner than it does in this country. I've a fair sum of money put by to take with us and wherever we settle down we can soon set ourselves up in the craft and perhaps even make our fortunes!'

'And we just disappear from here?'

'Yes, Seb, we just disappear!'


## A Score is Settled

The opportunity George Barker and his sons had been awaiting occurred during the university's Easter vacation when, early in the morning of the Wednesday preceeding Good Friday, Clarence Harding, as bold as brass, rode unaccompanied into the Swan Inn yard and left his horse at the stables in Timmy Ward's care. It was Sebastian who saw him ride by the forge and drew his father's attention to the incursion, pointing out at the same time that the usually busy yard was otherwise deserted.

'That's it then,' said the blacksmith putting down his hammer. 'As he passes here on foot on his way into the market place the three of us surround him and bring him into the forge.'

'And if he resists, father?'

'We clobber him, Seb, we clobber him!'

But their quarry made little effort to escape when the big man and his sturdy sons closed in upon him, contenting himself with saying, in a threatening voice, 'If you or these louts of yours harm me, smith, I'll have the law on you. My father will soon have the three of you in jail! So don't be fools! Let me go at once! Let me go, I say!'

'We're not letting you go,' said George Barker quietly. 'That is not until after we've finished with you. Then we'll let you free, then and only then!'

Thrust back against the rear wall of the forge with his wrists secured to rings in the brickwork, Clarence began to show signs of fear and his voice reached an hysterical pitch.

'I'm warning you, smith, I'm warning you!' he screamed. 'You'll all be going to prison for this!'

'Oh no, we shan't! We shan't be here to go! Now pay attention and listen!'

Clarence's screams gave way to a choked sobbing.

'You can hear me?'

'Yes! Yes!'

'You know why we've got you and why you've got to be punished?'

'You blame me for what happened to your daughter, don't you?'

'I do!'

'The court cleared me!'

'It did! But the court was wrong and you know it was. You and you alone are to blame for her disgrace and her death. Now we intend you to answer for what you did!'

George Barker stood back and then gave an order. 'Down with his breeches, boys, down with 'em round his ankles!'

'No! No! No!' Clarence began to kick out as his breeches were loosened and dragged down. 'No! No! No!' he cried.

'Yes! Yes! Yes!' said the smith and held up a knife so that Harding could see the light from the forge fire gleaming on its blade. 'Yes! Yes! Yes! You see this?'

The eyes of Clarence Harding opened wide in horror and realising that something terrible was about to happen to him, he began to scream.

'Gag him!' ordered George Barker. 'Gag him with his 'kerchief, Dave! Gag him tight as you can!'

David did as he had been bidden and then stepped backwards to survey the youth now struggling in silence.

'Not a pretty sight, is it boys? Not a pretty sight at all. Now one of you up with his shirt and the other holds his legs apart while I make sure he'll never rape another woman. Never ever!'

It took only seconds for the wielder of the knife to complete the severance. Having flung what he had cut away into the flames of the forge fire and put down his knife he took a long pair of tongs to draw from the fiercely glowing heart of the furnace a small round iron plate which was blindingly white with the heat. Slowly and deliberately he cauterised the gaping wound he had inflicted on the still conscious Harding and for several moments smoke and the sickly stench of burning flesh hung upon the air.

'You've killed him, father!' called out Sebastian as Harding's head fell forward and he ceased to struggle and to whimper beneath his gag.

'Oh no, I haven't. He's just fainted. What I have done will stop the sod bleeding to death, that's all. We don't want him dying on us do we? We want him to live on knowing what he will know when he comes to. Knowing that when it comes to womanising he's useless! Completely useless! He'll never have a son to inherit the title!

'And now we get out?'

'We do, Seb, we do. We take what we can carry with us and get away from Hitchin as quickly as we can.'

'And him?' Seb nodded in the direction of the suspended Harding. 'What about him?'

'Leave him where he is. The police can release him when they get my note.'

Barnabas received George Barker's missive just after midday. It had been brought to him at the police station by Timmy Ward who had demanded to see Inspector Tripp 'Urgent like!'

'Well?' queried Barnabas as Timmy stood before him in his office. 'What's so urgent, Timmy?'

'This, Sir, this!' a sealed envelope was held out for Barnabas to take. 'Mr Barker asked me to bring it to you but not until after church clock had struck twelve. Not afore, he said, and not long after. Said it were mighty important and you'd give me five shillin' when you read it. 'E gave me same so 'ere I am an' 'ere it is.'

It was a hurriedly written note which read –

*Barnabas,*

*Against your advice we have taken the law into our own hands and Clarence Harding will never do to any other woman what he did to our Sally. You will find him in the forge and you had best take a surgeon with you when you free him. We have no intention of answering to the law for what we have done and by the time you read this me and my two sons will be well on our way out of England and we are going where we shall never be found.*

*I am asking you as a friend and Masonic brother to sell what little we leave behind and pay off what we owe to the local tradesmen. Anything remaining you can drop into the Lodge Charity Box.*

*Yours fraternally*
*George Barker*

Barnabas looked up from his reading to see Timmy holding out a grimy open hand.

'Five shillin', please Sir,' he asked and Barnabas gave him a crown piece before dismissing him and sending for Sergeant Pearson. The sergeant with eyes agog, having read what had been written by the blacksmith said, 'Castrated him, have they?'

'Either that or cut something off a bit short!'

But when, with Dr Shillitoe by their side, they had lowered the then whimpering Clarence Harding on to a stretcher the three of them looked at each other appalled at what they could see.

'The whole damn lot!' said Shillitoe grimly. 'They've cut away the whole of his genitals! Now that does set me a problem!'

Sir Oliver Harding, red of face and short of temper, faced Barnabas in his study at Pirton Court and said angrily, 'I want them caught, Inspector, and I want them punished severely. What they did to that son of mine was barbaric and if I had my way they would hang for it!'

'We will catch them if we can, Sir, rest assured on that, but I fear we may be too late. They could be out of the country by now and on the high seas.'

'Then find out where they have gone or where they are making for. Have the rogues pursued!'

'We will continue to make enquiries, Sir. Strenuous enquiries. I can promise you that but as to pursuit beyond these shores, that I cannot promise.'

'Then get out and stay out! I see I'm to get little real help from you and I'll have to take the matter over your head. I've been told that Barker is one of those wretched Freemasons and it wouldn't surprise me if you were another!'

'Whether I am or whether I'm not, Sir, is no concern of yours and I shall do my duty irrespective of what you think. So, good day to you, Sir Oliver, good day to you!'

Barnabas picked up his cap, turned and briskly walked out of the booklined room.

Sir Oliver, when the door had closed behind the inspector, burst into tears.

It was to be ten years before Barnabas had any inkling of what had eventually happed to George Barker and his sons. A visitor to Hitchin from New Zealand commented in his hearing on the fine set of gates decorating the entrance to a house in Bancroft.

'I've only once seen a pair to equal them,' the bronzed man had said, 'Like 'em too!'

'And where was that?' Barnabas had asked.

'In Dunedin, Sir, opening up on a very nice garden. Made by one of our local smiths. Man with two sons also in the trade.'

'You don't know his name, I suppose?'

'Becker, I believe.'

'Not Barker?'

'No, George Becker. One of the sons is named Sebastian.'

'And,' Barnabas had said to himself, 'I'm pretty sure the name of the other son is David!'

# THE CASE OF THE
# KIDNAPPED SCHOOLGIRL

## The Kidnap

A few weeks after Clarence Harding's deprivation of what Sergeant Pearson referred to as his 'courting tackle' a short, slightly built man, but one whose bearing commanded respect, called early in the morning at the police station and quietly requested to see Inspector Tripp as soon as possible. Constable Hilton who was at the enquiries counter, recognising him at once said, 'Mr Rosen, isn't it, Sir, of the Three Gables in The Avenue?'

'It is. I am David Rosen, and my business with your inspector is both urgent and private. Is he available?'

'I'm sure he will be, Sir, when he knows it is you who wants to see him. Yes, Sir, quite sure!'

Hilton knocked at the closed inner office door and, having been bidden to enter, did so.

'Well?' queried Barnabas, looking up from the report he was writing, 'Well?'

'It's Mr Rosen, Sir. You know, the Jewish gentleman who lives in The Avenue. That big house there. He wants to see you quickly he does, and he says the matter is private!'

'Does he now? Well you'd best show him in here and make sure no one disturbs us for a while.'

'Yes, Sir, I'll bring him in, Sir.'

David Rosen, having removed his shining silk hat, quickly sat down opposite to Barnabas and said, as soon as he saw the door had been firmly closed, 'We have not met before, Inspector, and I regret having to trouble you now, Sir, but circumstances have arisen which compel me to seek your aid.'

'Those circumstances being what, Mr Rosen? They are obviously distressing ones by the look of grave concern on your face.'

'Yes. I am much distressed. My granddaughter has been kidnapped and a substantial ransom is being demanded for her release.'

'This is indeed serious, Sir.' Barnabas took a writing pad from a drawer in his desk and prepared to take notes. 'Her name, Sir, and her age?'

'Ruth. Ruth Rosen. She will be ten next birthday, which is fairly soon.'

'Her parents? Where are they?'

'Both dead, unfortunately. Drowned when *The Mirabelle* was sunk off the Newfoundland coast two years back. My wife was with them.'

'A terrible tragedy for you. So Ruth was left in your charge?'

'Yes. I am her guardian. She lives with me and attends daily the Academy for the Daughters of Gentlemen not far from here in Bancroft. Yesterday afternoon she did not return home but this missive was dropped through the letterbox about the time she should have done so.'

Rosen handed Barnabas a folded sheet of light blue paper and the inspector opened it to read –

*We have your granddaughter in our custody but she will come to no harm and we shall release her after payment to us of eight thousand pounds. You will be told how and when this will be handed over to us in a later communication. In the meantime you should not inform the police of this matter. If you do so you will regret it.*

*Revenge comes sweet to those who have been wronged, David Rosen.*

Barnabas, having laid the sheet of paper open on his desk, looked intently at the man with such a look of stress on his face.

'Do you recognise the writing? It is quite distinctive.'

'No, Inspector, I do not.'

'But you obviously have an enemy!'

'So it would seem but then a banker, such as myself, makes a number of enemies in the course of his business particularly when he has to foreclose on secured properties.'

'There is no person you can call to mind who might seek revenge in this cruel matter?'

'No, Inspector, nobody in particular.'

'No man? No woman?'

'Woman? Is that a possibility?'

'I think the handwriting of this demand is that of an educated woman. It is feminine, not masculine.'

David Rosen sat for a moment in silent thought. Eventually he shook his head and said, 'My direct dealings with women, Inspector, have been few and far between. I am a banker, not a pawnbroker dealing in jewellery, and I am at a complete loss. But now tell me, Sir, what do I do next?'

'You do nothing, Sir. There is nothing you can do until you get another communication. Then you bring this to us immediately. You seem quite prepared to ignore the threat in the first letter.'

'About approaching the police for help?'

'Yes. I am quite prepared to face the consequences of coming to you. I am also ready to pay the sum demanded. I am a very wealhty man, Inspector, and I can find the money fairly easily. I am certainly not prepared to allow the granddaughter I love to come to harm for what I consider a paltry sum.'

'I do not consider it to be a paltry sum, Mr Rosen, and I have every hope that you will not be called upon to pay it. If you are forced to do so we shall leave no stone unturned in our search for the kidnappers. I can assure you of that! The money must be recovered.'

'But the first priority must be to get Ruth back safe and sound. Is that not so?'

'It is. The money is of secondary consideration. Now please, let me call in my sergeant. He can note down the answers to some questions I would like to put to you.'

# Turning Stones

After Rosen had answered the questions asked of him concerning what Ruth had been wearing when she went to school that day, questions about her friends and acquaintances and questions about his household and servants, the banker left the police station still showing signs of great stress but at the same time giving the appearance of some relief at the thought that the matter was now in good and competent hands.

'We'll start with the Academy,' said Barnabas when the office door had closed behind Rosen. 'We must know, Sergeant, who saw the girl last before she disappeared. You and I will question the teachers and other pupils.'

'Very good, Sir, but may I make a suggestion?'

'Do, Sergeant, do.'

'Just in case any of our local rascals are involved in any way I think it may be well to have a few discreet enquiries made in Back Street. The girl could easily be hidden away in one of the slum yards. It's not impossible, is it, Sir?'

'No, it's not. Young Hilton has a contact there, hasn't he? See what he can find out. There might be a whisper of something as big as this afoot and it's certainly well worth trying. Tell him to be careful, extra careful. We don't want him kidnapped or worse!'

Pearson, having had a word or two with Hilton set off with Barnabas to the young ladies' Academy and enquiries there soon yielded a result. The formidable Madam Hardcastle who had recently taken over as headmistress quickly presented two girls, both in their early teens, who had seen Ruth getting into an enclosed carriage which had been waiting by the school gates near school closing time the day previous.

'Did she get into it willingly?' asked Barnabas.

'Yes,' replied the red-headed daughter of one of the town's leading lawyers, Penelope Hawkins, 'Quite willingly after someone inside, a woman, I think, spoke to her.'

'A woman? Can you describe her?'

Penelope hesitated and the other girl, eager to be better

noted, said, 'She looked like a proper lady, Sir. She was dressed all in black with a veil over her face. She was quite small.'

There was a nod of agreement from Penelope who added, 'So we couldn't properly see who she was but I'm sure she wasn't anybody we ought to have known, was she, Tilly?'

'Hm! That's disappointing,' said Barnabas, 'but what about the driver of the carriage? Did either of you take any notice of him?'

'I didn't,' said Penelope. 'I just didn't!'

'He was just a muffled up man,' said Tilly, 'sitting up on the box. There was nothing special about him.'

'Nothing at all?' asked Pearson, rather impatiently.

'Nothing!'

'Damn!' exclaimed Pearson, to be frowned upon immediately by Madam Hardcastle who said, 'Sergeant, you will please moderate your language. These are young ladies not used to hearing swear words. Not used at all!'

'Sorry, Ma'am. Very sorry! My apologies to the young ladies,' said Pearson contritely to receive, to his astonishment, a sly wink from Penelope with a silently mouthed, out of sight something which looked suspiciously like, 'Silly old bitch!'

Barnabas, aware of the interplay, said sharply, 'Now, one of you young ladies, please tell me which way the carriage was driven off. Towards the market square or towards the railway station?'

'Towards the railway station,' said Penelope, 'wasn't it Tilly?'

'Tilly nodded. 'Yes, but not fast or anything. The driver didn't seem to be in a hurry.'

With no more questions to ask, Barnabas and Sergeant Pearson returned to their own station. Over mugs of tea Pearson said, 'I don't suppose for a moment that the girl has been taken off by train but I do suppose we should make enquiries.'

'We will. No, Sergeant, my feeling is that she is being held somehwere to the north or east of the town.'

'Still in the town or beyond it, Sir?'

'Probably beyond it.'

'And the woman in the carriage? Do you think it was she who wrote that ransom demand?'

'Yes, I do and I wish we had a better description of her. So far we have nothing much to go on.'

Half an hour later when Constable Hilton reported to them they were still no better off. He said, 'There's no whisper in our Back Street area of a kidnapping and I've drawn a complete blank.'

'Then,' said Barnabas glumly, 'we shall have to await developments. There is nothing more we can do at the moment.'

# The Widow in Black

When, three months prior to the kidnapping, the Hitchin land and house agents Alcocks & Son, had been approached regarding furnished property to let in or near Hitchin they were able to offer the enquiring lady in black a detached house just on the outskirts of the village of Willian which seemed to meet her requirements in every possible way.

'Three large receptions rooms, four bedrooms and attic accommodation for your servants, also a large well equipped kitchen,' said John Alcocks persuasively, 'and the whole house attractively furnished in a modern fashion.'

'And stabling? I have my own carriage and pair.'

'The stabling and outbuildings are adequate, Madam, and there is a very pleasant garden. We can arrange local help with the garden maintenance.'

'And it is in a quiet, secluded place not overlooked by neighbours?'

'I can assure you of absolute privacy, Madam.'

'Then I should like to view the property.'

The next day the house had been inspected by the lady, who said her name was Emma Crighton and she was a widow, and a twelve months' tenancy was arranged at a very reasonable rent.

'The rent I shall pay in full in advance,' said Mrs Crighton, 'and that being so I take it, there will be no need for me to provide references?'

'No, Madam, no need at all and I hope your stay here will be a pleasant one.'

Within days Mrs Crighton moved into Highfield House with her housekeeper, the housekeeper's coachman and handyman husband and a young woman servant with an Irish accent.

Social callers were not encouraged. The Vicar's wife left her card, so too did the lady of the manor, Mrs Phipps-Brown, but no cards were left in exchange. Tradespeople called. The butcher, the baker and the local market gardener who sold fruit and vegetables. Groceries were delivered from the village shop and paid for on delivery much to the tradesman's delight. Whatever other shopping was done was not done in Hitchin but in Baldock. Hitchin seemed to be almost shunned by Mrs Crighton. Only very rarely was her carriage seen there. The villager, when speaking of her, referred to her as that 'Highfield widder-woman' and supposed her to be still grieving for a dead husband and choosing to do so in solitude.

Late in the evening of the third day following that of the kidnapping of Ruth Rosen Mrs Crighton rang the bell to summon her housekeeper to the small drawing room where she was seated at a side table on which were set out pens, ink and several sheets of pale blue writing paper.

'You rang, Ma'am,' queried the woman on her arrival in the room.

'I did, Sadie, I did. Two things. First, how is the girl settling down tonight? I take it that she has been put to her bed?'

'She has and she's making no bother at all. No paddy or tears tonight nor nothing. Brigid is with her and she's real taken to her she has.'

'Good! Now the second thing. This letter I've just written. Fetch that man of yours and I'll read it to you both.'

'He's not far off, Ma'am, in fact he's waiting in the hall just in case he might be wanted.'

'Then call him in.'

'I will,' said Sadie Jenkins.

On entering the room the surly looking Josiah Jenkins said gruffly, 'Well, I'm here, Mrs Crighton, and I'm listening.'

'Well, you and your wife listen carefully and both of you hold your tongues until I'm finished reading. Then if you've any comments I'll listen!'

'Fair enough! You just read what you've writ and if I don't like it I'll tell you. Same goes for Sadie as we're all in this together like. Right?'

'Yes, right.' Mrs Crighton began in a clear voice to read –

*David Rosen, We have reason to believe you have placed a certain matter in the hands of the police. Because this will mean extra trouble to us you will now pay us ten thousand, not eight thousand pounds.*

*You will put this into four leather bags and take these to London on the 1.22 train from Hitchin on Saturday. You may have a manservant to assist you in carrying the bags. At Kings Cross you will be met off the train by our agent and given further instructions.*

*Ruth is at present unharmed and well and she will remain so unless you fail to do as we now require or if you attempt to have our agent and the money followed up in London. When the agent and the money are safely in our hands Ruth will be set free.*

At the conclusion of her reading Emma Crighton put down the letter and looking as Josiah Jenkins asked, 'Well?'

'Well enough,' replied the man, 'I can't fault it, I can't and now Rosen'll know there's several of us in it. And that extra two thousand, you'll be giving me an' the wife half of that, won't you?'

'I shall. You and Sadie will now be getting three thousand between you.'

The man's eyes glittered avariciously as he hissed, 'Three lovely thousand! Three lovely, bloody thousand!' Turning to his wife he said, 'We can set ourselves up quite well on that, can't we Sadie? Real well!'

Sadie smiled her thin lipped smile. 'Yes, real well, husband. We'll find a nice little inn to buy in a nice little place and have nothing to worry about for the rest of our lives.' Turning to Mrs Crighton she added, 'And you'd better give Brigid some extra. She's worked wonders with Miss Uppity, she has.'

'She'll get something more and I shall pay her off as soon as we have released the girl, with orders to go back to Ireland immediately. She knows too much and if the police do get on our track I don't want her questioned. The sooner she is across the water the better. Now to another matter—'

'Yes, what's that?' asked Josiah Jenkins.

'That storage place in Kentish Town under the railway arches. I take it that you were able to rent it?'

'I was. For a month. No problem.'

'Good! Then you can post this letter tomorrow morning at the Hitchin post box. It should reach Rosen by the afternoon.'

'And when he reads what's writ he'll have something to think about, won't he?'

'He will! He certainly will. He'll have even more to think about when he parts with his money!'

Josiah Jenkins grinned. 'He sure won't like it!' he said and then went on to ask, 'We come back here when we've got it?'

'We shall have to. The girl has to be released and Brigid paid off and put on the train.'

'And then, Mrs Crighton?'

'You'll take me to Harwich and we'll part company there. You'll go on your way and I shall go mine over the water.'

'Yes, Mrs Crighton, you'll go on your way and we shall go ours.' Bus as Josiah was saying this he was turning over in his mind an idea which had occurred to him. It was an idea which if acted upon would lead to a far from amicable parting.

❖ ❖ ❖ ❖ ❖

## Amen to a Prayer

The letter was received by David Rosen at his house in The Avenue in mid afternoon and was immediately taken to the police station.

'An extra two thousand pounds!' exclaimed Barnabas on reading it. 'That's steep! Damned steep!'

'But it's not of great consequence,' said Rosen calmly. 'No consequence at all.'

'And you can raise ten thousand in gold sovereigns by Saturday? You have only three day to do so, Sir.'

'It will not be difficult,' said the banker, 'but it is something of a nuisance having so large and weighty a sum brought down from London on the Friday only to be taken back again the next day. However, I think we had better do exactly what is laid down in the letter. We may be under surveillance and I do not want Ruth to be put at any more risk than she already is.'

'I agree, but I do have a suggestion to make,' said Barnabas.

'Which is, Inspector?'

'That instead of taking one of your servants to assist you, you take one of my constables in footman's livery. I have someone in mind who is not only young and strong but also highly intelligent and resourceful.'

'Hilton?' murmured Pearson.

'Yes, Sergeant, Hilton! I'm sure you'll agree that he's the right man to go with Mr Rosen.'

'I do agree, Sir, fully!'

'Then I accept your suggestion gladly,' said David Rosen, 'but what I am not easy in my mind about is that the letter makes no mention of how Ruth is to be exchanged for the money.'

'True, Sir,' replied Barnabas, 'it doesn't, but unfortunately we are in no position to demand any form of guarantee. We are being held over a barrel and there is precious little we can do about it. Once Ruth is safely back with you we may be able to do something about the recovery of the money but until she is we must proceed with the utmost caution. We shall certainly have you and Hilton under observation when contact is made at Kings Cross station but after that I doubt if we can do very much.'

'You won't attempt to follow us?'

'Only if we think we can do so without being seen. Even in London following you unobserved could be difficult.'

'Then, Inspector, we must all pray and pray hard for the safe return of Ruth.'

Barnabas nodded grimly and Sergeant Pearson muttered, 'Amen to that, Sir, Amen.'

## Captured

The train from Hitchin drew into Platform 6 at Kings Cross exactly at its due time. The arrival was witnessed by Barnabas and Sergeant Pearson who, in plain clothes, stood at a discreet distance from the ticket collection barrier to see Rosen and Hilton pass through and what contact was to be made with the heavily laden pair.

Person nudged Barnabas. 'It's going to be her, Sir,' he murmured, indicating a veiled woman in dark clothing who had moved close to the barrier and was closely scanning the passing through passengers.

'Yes, Sergeant, I'm sure you're right but it is not the same woman who took the girl off from the school. Penelope Hawkins said she was a small lady. This one is quite tall and, to my mind, not quite a lady. More a servant.'

'Yes, Sir, but it is the one we want at the moment. Look, she's approached Mr Rosen and he and Hilton are following her along the concourse.'

Keeping a fair distance between them and their quarry, Barnabas and Pearson followed the trio to the side exit from the station which opened out almost into the forecourt of the recently erected Great Northern Hotel. There a closed carriage was waiting with a driver up on his seat. A driver who called out something and raised his whip when he saw the woman and the two men approaching the carriage.

'He's telling them to hurry,' said Pearson, 'and they'll be off and away long before we can do anything about following them!'

And it was only moments, before, with its passengers aboard, the carriage was merging into the traffic of a side street.

'Damn!' said Pearson. 'There's no chance of catching up with them, bugger it! No bloody chance at all!'

'We've no need to!' said Barnabas.

'No need, Sir?'

'Yes! No need. We've Hilton aboard with Rosen and the money and we can rely on them to give us a full report when we get them back.'

'If we do get them back, Sir!'

'I'm sure we shall. I doubt if murder is in the mind of the kidnappers, Sergeant. Murder is not their game.'

'I hope you're right, Sir, but where do you think they are making for?'

'I've no idea at all. There is a welter of narrow streets and hidey holes north of here. Somers Town, Camden Town, Kentish Town, even Hampstead. All within easy reach!'

'So all we can do is wait?'

'Yes, we return to Hitchin and wait!'

In the carriage little was said. An enquiry from Rosen as to where they were going was ignored. Asked if Ruth would be exchanged immediately in return for the gold the woman said gruffly, 'You'll know everything in good time. Don't try anything now or when we get where we're going. See!' She produced an ugly looking revolver from under her muff and pointed it at Rosen's head. 'It is loaded,' she said, 'and I do know how to use it!'

'Yes, Madam, I'm sure you do and we have no intention of trying anything now or later. That would be foolish on our part.'

'Indeed it would. Very foolish!'

Nothing more was said and the carriage, moving at a fair speed passed along a number of mean streets. Only occasionally did Rosen or Hilton catch a glimpse of a street name through the carriage windows and those they did see were meaningless.

Eventually the carriage slowed down and turned into a

gloomy cobbled yard bounded on one side by a series of half a dozen railway arches all of which had been strongly boarded off with inset doors to provide covered storage accommodation units.

When the carriage had come to a gentle halt the woman said sharply, 'We're here! Pick up your bags, you two, get out and stand by that doorway numbered four. Then wait for me to join you.'

Rosen and Hilton did as they had been ordered. Both took the opportunity of looking around but learned little. Beyond the carriage and its occupants the yard was deserted. It was bounded on three sides by high walls broken only by the gateway of their entrance. A train rumbled by over the archways and broke the curiously depressing silence of the area. As the rumbling died away they were joined by the coachman and the veiled woman. The reins of the horses had been hitched to a ring set in the brickwork of the arches. It was the woman who opened the door and ushered them through, at pistol point, into the vault beyond.

There at the far end, seated at a table on which there were two lit candle, was another veiled woman. This one was quite small and elegantly dressed. When she spoke her voice was soft and cultivated. She said, 'You and your man, Mr Rosen, can come forward and place your bags on this table, please.'

Before complying with her request Rosen peered around him and asked, 'Where is Ruth? Is she not here? I fully expected to exchange her at once for the money in the bags.'

'You did, did you? Well she would have been handed over at once had you not brought in the police and made the transaction more difficult than it need have been. No we cannot release her until tomorrow but she will be freed in Hitchin not far from her home. That I do promise you.'

'But who, Madam, are you and why should I believe you will do as you say you will?'

'You will have to believe me, Rosen, and as to who I am you would not know me even if I removed my veil. Let it suffice that it was you who ruined my husband. He need not have been ruined if you had allowed him a few extra days before foreclosing on his estate. He could not face ruin and shot himself with the revolver which is now being pointed at you. Fortunately I was not left destitute and since his death I have been able to live modestly abroad while I planned this revenge. Not only have I been able to cause you concern and distress but I am now taking sufficient of your money to amply repay two faithful servants who have helped me, with enough left to keep me in greater comfort for the remainder of my days.'

'Yes, Madam, you have caused me distress and I do resent paying the ransom you have demanded. Do you wish to count the money?'

'No. I do not. Just place the bags on this table, then the pair of you step back together. When we leave we shall lock you up in here and there is the best part of a dozen candles left in the box under the table to light you through until you are released sometime tomorrow.'

'Tomorrow! But who will release us then?'

'Who, Rosen, who? Probably your friends the police. You see when we set the girl free she will be carrying a note giving details of your whereabouts. She will also have the key to the padlock on the door.'

'You seem to have thought of everything!'

'We have tried to do so. You will even find some bottles of beer, a loaf of bread and some cheese in the box with the candles!'

The driver of the carriage who hitherto had been silent, broke in with an unpleasant chortle to add offensively, 'Yes, and a bloody knife as well. What's more you've even got straw in that corner over there for making yourselves a bed tonight, though how you're going to sleep with the trains rattling over you I don't know and don't want to know!' Having said this the man picked up two of the bags of gold and made for the door. The tall woman, having handed the revolver to the one who seemed to be her mistress, followed him with the other two bags.

Then, standing, the small woman indicated with the gun that Rosen and Hilton should move over to the wall on their right.

'Now turn about and face it!' she ordered as, moving backwards, she went to the door and made her own exit.

After they had heard the door slammed closed Rosen said, 'Well, Hilton, here we are and here we stay, whether we like it or not.'

'Yes, Sir, we're trapped and all to no purpose. The money has gone but we haven't got Miss Ruth and we don't seem to have learned very much.'

'But I do know one thing, Constable!'

'And what is that, Sir?'

'I know who is behind the kidnapping and our present predicament!'

'You know the small woman's name?'

'I do! She is or was a Mrs Partington. She probably calls herself something else these days in view of Partington's disgrace and suicide a few years back.'

'The Partington Bank fraud and scandal?'

'Yes! Hundreds were ruined and Partington took his own life rather than face up to a long prison sentence. Where the investors' money went was never discovered but it was thought likely he had gambled it away in Monte Carlo. Fortunately my own bank had the security of his small estate in Bedfordshire and we were able to recover the loan made to him. It was our foreclosure on this which precipitated the disaster which led to his downfall. Somehow or other he must have had funds salted away in his wife's name and it is on these she must have been living while she planned revenge on me. It was a revenge which was to include payment to her of a substantial sum of money.'

'You did not challenge her with any of this, Sir?'

'No, I didn't, Constable. I thought it unwise to let her know I was aware of her identity. That driver of hers has the look of a real villain about him. If she had told him to silence the pair of us for good I don't doubt he would have done so willingly!'

'You're probably right, Sir, and we've had a lucky escape. One thing we do have is a good description of him and I noticed one thing in particular.'

'What was that, Constable?'

'He's short of three fingers on his left hand. All three are missing completely and a mutilated hand like that is very noticeable. It is something we can ask about when we start making enquiries.'

'Yes, Hilton, you are right. It should provide a very useful lead but for the time being I think we had better concern ourselves with having a meal and bedmaking. Thank goodness that straw looks dry!'

But neither Rosen or Constable Hilton got much sleep that night. The trains were frequent and the straw was full of fleas.


## Call me Bridie

The first two days of Ruth Rosen's captivity had been trying ones with much screaming and many tears. On the third day however she had claimed down considerably and a warm and pleasant relationship began to develop between her and the wide eyed, open faced young Irish woman who was her somewhat reluctant gaoler.

When Ruth's midday meal had been served on a tray the woman stood back smiling to say, in her soft brogue, 'I hope you'll enjoy that, Miss Ruth, it's a nice little piece of roast chicken, with roast praties and beans from the garden. Just the same as I've served the lady of the house with a few minutes ago and there'll be some jam pudding and custard to follow. You'll like that, indeed I'm sure you will!'

Ruth, smiling in return, said, 'Thank you. Everything does look nice but tell me—'

'Tell you what? I will if I can.'

'Tell me first what I should call you, then tell me about the lady downstairs and tell me why I am being kept here!'

'That's a lot of tell me, isn't it, Miss Ruth, but for a start my name is Brigid Murphy but my friends call me Bridie. I hope you'll call me that. Yes, you call me Bridie.'

'I will, Bridie. It's a pretty name. Pretty, like you!'

Bridie blushed. 'Thank you, Miss Ruth, but there's lots prettier than me where I come from. But enough of that. Now about the lady downstairs. I mustn't tell you her name. Nor am I supposed to tell you the name of the housekeeper nor that of her husband who does general work about the house and the stables and drives the carriage or the pony and trap. Not that I think they are their real names, I don't!'

'Well, Bridie, if you can't tell me what they call themselves perhaps you can tell me why I have been shut up here. My grandfather will be very worried about me and I want to go home.'

'I 'spect you do, Miss Ruth, but them downstairs say you can't be sent home until that grandfather of yours has paid over the money he owes to the lady.'

'Grandfather doesn't owe anybody any money. He's a very rich man and doesn't need to. He pays everybody for what he has! Quickly! As soon as he has it!'

'Well, that's not what they say downstairs. As soon as he does pay them they'll let you go and they'll give me enough money for looking after you to do what I want to do.'

'What do you want to do, Bridie?'

'Go back to Ireland with enough in my purse to pay for ma and me and my two brothers to go on a ship to America.'

'Where's your father?'

'He's already in America. He's got work there on the railway. Now that's enough questions, Miss Ruth, for the moment so please get on with your meal and when you've done you an' me will have a game of cards and then I'll show you how to build a house with them.'

'I know how to build a house with cards! And how to knock it down! No, you see if you can find some draughts in the house and a board and I'll teach you how to play. Draughts is better than cards! Lots better!'

And so it was the following days were not passed too unpleasantly for the kidnapped girl and her gaoler. Then early in the morning of the day the ransom money was to be collected, Emma Crighton sent for Bridie and in the presence of Josiah and Sadie Jenkins gave her instructions regarding the custody of Ruth during their absence.

'You'll give her a meal at the normal time and have something yourself. Mrs Jenkins has left two covered plates on the kitchen table and there's fruit to follow.'

'Yes, Ma'am.'

'Good! Expect us to return about seven this evening.'

'Yes, Ma'am, about seven.'

'On no account is she to be allowed out of her room even though we are not here. You understand that, Bridie?'

'Yes, Ma'am, I understand that.'

'Good, again! Tomorrow or the day after you'll be leaving here and returning to Ireland where you're to disappear.'

'Yes, Ma'am, and you'll be giving me the money you said you would?'

'Yes, with a little extra for being a good young woman.'

'Thank you, Ma'am, thank you very much. I shall never forget you, never!'

'The sooner you forget us and what has happened here the better, Bridie. You must tell no one about us or where you have been. If anyone does ask just say you have been in service in England and that you had a generous mistress.'

'Yes, Ma'am, that's what I'll say.'

'Good! Now go back to the girl. We shall be leaving shortly. All being well we shall return at the time I said.'

Twenty minutes later the carriage left for London.


## The Return and a Sudden Death

It was in fact only a little after six o'clock when Emma Crighton and the two Jenkins returned to Highfield House in the now gold laden carriage. The arrival was watched with interest by Ruth and Bridie from the high up dormer window of Ruth's room in the wing of the house.

'They're back a lot earlier than she told me that they would be,' said Bridie, 'and I reckon the driver's a bit tiddley like,' she added, as she saw Jenkins stagger up the front doorsteps with two obviously heavy bags, urged on by a following wife who was also carrying two bags.

'Tiddley?' queried Ruth. 'Do you mean drunk, Bridie?'

'Not real drunk, just tiddley and he's not nice when he gets like that. I've seen him like it once before and I reckon I'd best slip down and watch from behind the scenes just in case he turns on his wife and I have to help her again.'

But it was not his wife that Jenkins turned upon after the four bags of gold had been deposited in the study but his mistress, Emma Crighton.

'Stand aside, you bitch!' he shouted. 'It's two of them bags we're having! Not one. Half each and that's plenty for you and enough for us and I'm taking ours now!'

Emma Crighton said calmly, 'Quiet, you drunken fool. You've been drinking ever since we gave the horses a break at Hatfield. You bought a bottle of brandy at the inn, didn't you?'

'What if I did, you old cow?'

'You've been swigging at it the rest of the way back, haven't you?'

Jenkins glared bleary eyed at his questioner. 'Aye, woman, I've had a nip or two but I'm not that far gone, and whether you like it or whether you don't, half of what's there is going with Sadie an' me!'

Through the crack of the door behind which she was hiding, Bridie saw Jenkins reaching forward to the bags and as he did so Emma Crighton produced the revolver from her muff. She said firmly, 'Stand back Jenkins or I'll put a bullet in your belly and you won't live to take anything!'

'You wouldn't dare, you besom, you wouldn't dare!'

As he shouted this Jenkins flung himself forward to grab Emma Crighton's hand and twist it so that the muzzle of the gun was pressed into her bosom. The sound of a shot followed immediately and with a look of astonishment on her face and a bubble of bright red blood on her lips the woman fell sideways into a crumpled heap on the carpet.

'You've killed her, you fool! shouted Sadie Jenkins. 'You'll swing for it! You've murdered her, you have!'

Josiah Jenkins, shocked into near sobriety, stared down at the corpse. 'It weren't murder,' he said shakily. 'She pulled the trigger herself! Weren't me did it!'

'Police won't take no account of that, nor will judge and jury. It'll still count as murder and you'll hang for it if you're caught! Hang high, you will!'

'And you'll like as not hang with me if we're took but I'm going to make sure we ain't took by bloody police.'

'How?'

'How, woman, how? They won't even know about us and the kidnapping or anything else much if we do away with the two upstairs!'

'The girl and Bridie?'

'Them two. Both of them. It's the only sure way to stop them talking!' Josiah picked up the pistol from where it had fallen and Sadie looked at him aghast.

'But you can't kill them in cold blood, Josiah!'

'I can and I will as soon as we've taken these bags to the carriage ready for a quick getaway afterwards. All this gold is ours now, woman, you realise that don't you? Ours! Ours! Ours!'

Bridie had overheard enough. Terrified she made for the stairs, her mind concentrating on an idea which had occurred to her. At the top of the stairs she went to the door of the room in which Ruth was confined. Pushing back the heavy bolt she opened the door and called out, calmly enough, 'It's only me, my dear, only me.'

'Bridie! Bridie!' The girl inside rushed quickly towards her seeking comfort in the young Irish woman's embrace and asking, 'What was that noise I heard just now? It sounded like a gun going off, was it?'

'It was, Ruth, and something terrible has happened downstairs. Real terrible. And something real terrible will happen to us if we don't do something quick and escape!'

'What have we got to do, Bridie?'

'You trust me?'

'Yes, Bridie, I trust you.'

'Good! I want you to hide in the cupboard on the landing outside and be absolutely still and quiet there no matter what you hear happening. When it's safe for you to come out I'll open the door and we'll run off together and find a policeman as soon as we can! You understand?'

Ruth stood back from Bridie and nodded solemnly but with eyes bright with excitement. She said, 'I'm to hide in the cupboard and be quiet until you let me out. That's it, isn't it Bridie?'

'It is! Quick! Out with you on to the landing and into the cupboard! Now!'

When Ruth was in the cupboard Bridie went back into the child's room and having flung the window wide open began to scream loudly. The Jenkins, returning to the study after loading the gold and a few personal possessions in the carriage, heard the screams and with Josiah, pistol in hand leading, the pair of them rushed up the stairs to find Bridie by the door of Ruth's room pointing across this to the open window on its far side.

Bridie ceased her screaming to shout, 'She's gone! Ruth's gone! She's out on the roof! She's gone!' Jenkins and his wife pushed by her with the man swearing profusely and the woman gabbling something which sounded like a string of curses. Both turned and were suddenly silent when they heard the door behind them being slammed shut and the bolt on the other side being driven home by Bridie.

Two bullets from Josiah Jenkins's pistol punctured a panel of the stout door but by the time these were fired Bridie and Ruth were off the landing and on their way downstairs.

## Loose Ends

Josiah Jenkins glared first at the close bolted door, secondly at the pistol in his hand and lastly, with reluctance, at the open window.

'Shoot away that bolt,' suggested his wife. 'You know where it is on the other side of the door. You put it there!'

'I know I put it there, woman, and I know there's no bloody chance of shooting it away with what I've got left in this gun. No bloody chance at all!'

'Then what? Do we stay here until we rot or get picked up by the police?'

'We bloody don't, we . . .'

Jenkins stopped speaking and rushed back to the window from which he could see the carriage standing by the front entrance to the house. 'Sod it!' he said, 'and sod that bloody Irish cow! Do you know what she's doing now?'

'What?'

'She's up on the box with the girl by her side and getting ready to drive off!'

'With the gold?'

'Yes, woman! With all the gold! The whole bloody lot of it!'

Taking aim with the pistol the frustrated man fired three times at the carriage but to no effect other than a slight splintering of the woodwork of one door. He threw down the empty pistol in disgust as, with a clattering of hooves and the fierce crunching of wheels in the gravel, Bridie drove off the carriage at speed.

'Gone! They've bloody gone!' shouted Jenkins. 'Bloody gone!'

'Now what do we do?' wailed Sadie bursting into tears.

'A lot! We ain't finished yet, not by a long chalk. I'm going out through that window and along the roof to where the house is joined by the outbuildings. I'll lower myself on to them and then go down a drainpipe to the ground. I'll come back through the house and let you out. There's still a pony and trap in the stables for us to use and we'll take with us what jewellery and money we can lay hands on and bugger off quick. The old bitch had a lot of sparklers which must be worth quite a bit and we'll be fools if we leave anything of value behind.'

With some difficulty Jenkins eased himself out of the dormer window and clambered up on to the slated roof. Choosing not to stand he quickly worked his way on his buttocks to the turn in the roof and then beyond the turn until he was directly above the main entrance to the house. There disaster struck. He began slithering towards the edge of the roof among a number of loose slates. Within moments, despite his frantic efforts to save himself, he was over the edge. For a second or so he clung desperately at the gutter with one hand, the maimed one. The thumb and the solitary finger were not enough to sustain his weight and with a loud scream and wildly kicking legs he plunged to the ground thirty feet below. There, face downward in the gravel of the drive, he lay sprawled and ominously silent.

Sadie, who had heard his scream and witnessed his fall, stood back from the window and began to sob.

Barnabas looked up from his desk to regard the office clock with concern plain upon his face. Sergeant Pearson who was with him turned on his chair and also looked up at the clock. He said, 'It's gone half six and they should be back by now, Sir, or we should have heard from them, surely? They could have used the Post Office telegraph and got a message through if they were being delayed for some reason, couldn't they?'

'They could and should have done and it worries me, Sergeant. All we know is they were contacted by the kidnappers and driven off somewhere in London. Where they are and whether or not they've got the girl safe and sound we just don't know.'

'No, Sir, nor whether the two of them are safe and sound themselves. We just don't know but I do know I've a deal of faith in young Hilton . . .'

Before he could say more a carriage came to an abrupt and noisy standstill in front of the office window and both inspector and sergeant rose quickly to their feet to get a better view.

'Curious,' said Barnabas. 'A woman up on the box with no cloak or bonnet and a young girl beside her!'

Pearson cried out, 'And I reckon I know who the girl is!'

'Who?'

'The one we're looking for, Sir! Rosen's granddaughter!'

'You're likely right! She's about the right age and dark haired!' Then Barnabas added as he saw Bridie clamber quickly down from her seat and hasten to help Ruth down to the ground, 'And whoever it is who has brought her in is in a hurry to tell us all about it, by the look of things!'

Less than a minute later the flustered Bridie and the excited girl were brought through to the office by the desk constable and even as she was entering through the doorway the young Irish woman was beginning to pour out her story to the much intrigued police officers.

When, still standing, she had come to the end of her only semi-coherent account of the happenings at Highfield House, Barnabas, calm and reassuring, suggested that she and the girl be seated while he and the sergeant asked a few questions. When they were occupying chairs the inspector looked at Bridie and asked her name.

'Bridie, Sir, Bridie Mahony.'

'Good, Bridie, and from what you have been telling me I gather you were employed by a Mrs Crighton as a general servant at Highfield House at Willian?'

'Yes, Sir, general servant. There were two other servants. Mr and Mrs Jenkins. She was the housekeeper and he was the handyman and coachdriver.'

'And you say you were offered extra money to look after Ruth here when she was kidnapped?'

'Yes, Sir. Enough money to pay for me and my ma and my brother and sister to go to 'Merica on a ship. Mrs Crighton said they weren't going to hurt Miss Ruth, only keep her until her grandfather had repaid some money he had stolen from Mr Crighton who was now dead.'

'You believed her?'

'I did, Sir. She weren't bad or nasty or anything, like Mr and Mrs Jenkins were.'

'And you say you saw Mr Jenkins shoot Mrs Crighton?'

'Yes, Sir, I did. I saw him do it through a crack in the door. Shoot her he did! And I ran off 'cos he said he was going to shoot me and Ruth to stop us telling about it and them.'

'And you've trapped the two of them in an attic room?'

'Bolted them in, I did!'

'Good! And so you were able to escape to the carriage and drive down to here?'

'Yes, Sir, that's right Sir!'

'You're a good, brave young woman, Bridie, and I don't doubt Ruth's grandfather will reward you properly for what you've done. You've saved his granddaughter's life and saved him a great deal of money.' Barnabas paused, 'I don't suppose you heard anything about what happened in London when the gold was picked up? Ruth's grandfather and one of my constables who was with him at the handover seem to have disappeared.'

Bridie shook her head. 'No, Sir,' she said, 'nobody said nothing about London. Nothing.'

'You're sure?'

'Absolutely sure, Sir. Nothing.'

Disappointed, Barnabas turned to Ruth and said, 'Now young lady, I think the best thing to do with you is to get you home as soon as possible and that we'll do!'

'Can Bridie come home with me, please, Mr Policeman? I'm sure my grandfather won't mind her staying at our house after all she did for me. He won't mind at all.'

Barnabas smiled and said, 'I'm sure he won't, Ruth and Bridie can't very well return to Highfield House, can she?'

'No, Mr Policeman, she can't and I don't want her to! So there!'

'That's settled then, Bridie will go home with you, and the sergeant here and I will go to Willian and attend to matters there.'

Ruth looked solemnly at Barnabas and then said, 'You'll look after the money, will you Mr Policeman, and keep it in a safe place?'

Both Barnabas and Sergeant Pearson laughed. 'We will!' said Barnabas. 'We shall take it into custody and lock it away in one of our cells! It will be very safe there!'

The first thing the two police officers noticed as they rounded the bend in the drive at Highfield House was the still body of man sprawled on the gravel not far from the front door of the small mansion. As they rode nearer the corpse they could see the surrounding broken slates and looking up to the roof and seeing a dangling length of gutter they realised what had happened.

Having dismounted and turned the body face uppermost Pearson said, 'Jenkins, I suppose, Sir?'

'I would think so, Sergeant, and he must have fallen in an attempt to escape from the attic by climbing along the roof until he could find some means of getting to the ground.'

'Well, the fall has saved Jack Ketch from the job of hanging him for murder!'

'And, Sergeant, saved us a deal of trouble and paperwork! Now we'd better have a look in the house. The library first and make sure Mrs Crighton is dead.'

'They quickly found the room and the body.

'She's dead all right,' said Pearson after a quick examination of the corpse during which he closed the dead woman's eyes. 'The bullet must have gone straight through the heart and she couldn't be deader!'

They also had no difficulty in finding the attic in which the half hysterical Sadie Jenkins was confined.

'Let me out!' she was shouting as the door was opened.'Let me out! It was him who did it! Not me!'

Sergeant Pearson, who had unbolted the door, found himself being overwhelmed and pushed to one side by the screaming woman. Only with difficulty and the assistance of Barnabas was she forced back into the room and seated in a chair. Then to quieten her, Pearson slapped her face. This brought silence and a flood of tears. When this showed signs of ceasing Barnabas asked, 'You're Mrs Jenkins, aren't you?'

With red, wet eyes, the woman glared up at him to say, 'What if I am?'

'Your husband is dead!'

'I know! I saw him fall off the roof!'

'You were present when he shot Mrs Crighton, weren't you?'

'That was an accident. He didn't mean to kill her. Didn't mean to at all and it wouldn't have happened if she had let us have our proper share of the money!'

'We know about the kidnap money and it is now in our possession but we don't know what has happened to Mr Rosen and our constable in London. Where are they? We want some information out of you.'

The tears gave way completely to a cunning smile and a taunting, 'You do, do you?'

'Yes, we do!'

'It'll count for me if I tell you where they are?'

'No bargains but it won't count against you if you do co-operate. Of that I can assure you.'

'Can you, Inspector? Good! Then I'll tell you. Kentish Town. That's where they are. Locked up!'

'Kentish Town is a big area. Where in Kentish Town?'

'Cobb Yard. Off Caversham Street. In a railway arch storage place. Number four and the key to the padlock on the door should be in my husband's pocket. It's strung on a wood tab.'

'It is now? On a wood tab you say?'

'Yes, Inspector, a big wood tab with a number burnt on it.'

Barnabas turned from the woman to Sergeant Pearson and grinned. He said, 'A nice little job for you, I think, Sergeant.'

'Yes, Sir, a very nice little job for me. I've to get the key, ride into Hitchin, take the next train to Kings Cross and then get a cab to Cobb Yard. Correct, Sir?'

'Yes, Sergeant, and when you've released them—'

'I bring them back to Hitchin Police Station, Sir!'

'Yes! No matter what time it is, Sergeant!'

The amused Pearson jerked a thumb in the direction of Sadie Jenkins. 'And what about her?' he asked.

'By now the station wagonette should be outside with two men. They can take her off and lock her up in the cell next to the one containing the gold. Tomorrow I'll have her brought up before the magistrates.'

'And that, Sir, if I may say so, will be a very nice tidying up of the last of some very nasty loose ends!'

'It will, Sergeant, it will indeed!'

# A Birthday Party and
# Wedding Bells for Arthur Hilton

Ruth Rosen's eleventh birthday occurred three weeks exactly after her safe return home and to mark the occasion and as a thanksgiving her grandfather arranged a celebratory tea party in the garden of his home to which he invited more than eighty guests. These included not only a number of Ruth's school friends, a bevy of London cousins but also his doctor and his family, his lawyer and his family and the police officers who had helped in the search for his granddaughter together with their families.

Dressed in their finery and thankful it was a really lovely afternoon, Barnabas and Laura with their three children set off for Rosen's house in the residential quarter of the town in a large, open carriage especially hired for the occasion.

'Musn't be too early,' observed Laura as the carriage reached the corner by the Walsworth Road Baptist Chapel, 'that's embarrassing and we must not be late, that's rude! We must arrive at the reception at exactly the right time!'

'That is what we shall do,' said Barnabas with a smile looking down at the large silver watch he had taken from his pocket, 'and we arrive in good company too. There, on the path, are Sergeant and Mrs Pearson and their two and Hilton is with them. A very smart looking Hilton too!'

Foiling an attempt by his younger daughter to grab his watch Barnabas laughed and restored it to his pocket. Patricia Laura pouted prettily and then gave her father a devastating smile. She was a very good natured child although spoilt by her brother, her sister and both parents who all adored her.

'Minx!' said Barnabas. 'You get more and more like you mother every day!'

'Better like me than like you, you great hulk!' said Laura, chuckling, before gathering up her youngest and murmuring, 'Don't you dare grow up, my pet, to be as tall as that father of yours or we shall never be able to marry you off when it's time to do so. Never, ever!'

Having told the driver of the carriage to return and pick them up at half past the hour of six Barnabas helped Laura and the children down to the pavement and then began ushering them towards the gaily decorated gateway of Three Gables House. There they were joined by the Pearsons and Constable Hilton.

'Bit of a crush, Sir,' said the sergeant as they began to mingle with guests also making their entry and on their way to where, on the closely shaven lawn, a large marquee had been erected.

'Yes,' agreed Barnabas. 'Certainly a crush but a happy one and it looks as though Mr Rosen is doing us proud today. I can even hear a small orchestra playing in the background.'

David Rosen and his granddaughter were waiting by the entrance to the marquee to receive their guests and when Barnabas and his family reached them Rosen drew Barnabas to one side to ask quietly, 'Anything fresh to report, Inspector?'

'Not much, Sir, Mrs Jenkins is likely to be brought up for trial in about a month's time and you will shortly be notified of the date you'll be wanted to give your evidence. Secondly we have been able to find a close, male relative of Emma Crighton's and his solicitor is now in the process of clearing up her estate.'

'Good! And Bridie? Brigid Mahony?'

'No charges Sir, but she has to remain in this country until after the trial of Mrs Jenkins. She will be the principal witness for the prosecution. She is still with you, I hope, Sir?'

'She is, Inspector. Very much so, and I hope you will have a word with her before you leave today. It will put her mind at rest. She is over there serving lemonade to our guests.'

'I will, Sir, I will. As soon as it is convenient I will speak to her.'

After their gaily wrapped present had been handed over to the blushing Ruth Barnabas and his family moved on to merge with the other guests and to enjoy the various diversions provided in the garden which included a treasure hunt, a skittle alley and a coconut shy. At four o'clock, with Daniel proudly carrying the coconut his father had knocked down, the five of them adjourned to the marquee for a meal. There, while Barnabas and Laura enjoyed cups of tea and a variety of delicious sandwiches and pastries, their children tucked into lemonade, trifles, jellies, and cakes to their hearts' and stomachs' content. There was even ice cream!

During a slight lull in the demand for lemonade Barnabas had his word with Bridie.

'So I don't have anything to worry about, Sir,' she said after hearing what he had to say.

'No, Bridie, you don't. Just tell the judge and jury what you told us and that's all that will be needed from you.'

'Yes, Sir, I'll do that. Thank you. Has Mr Rosen told you what he has done for me already?'

'No, Bridie, he hasn't. What has he done?'

'He's sent enough money or Ireland to pay for all of my family there to go to America, and something to live on when they get there.'

'That is very generous of him but what about you? Don't you want to join them over there when the trial is over?'

Bridie shook her head and looked fixedly across the marquee where Ruth Rosen was talking to Mrs Hardcastle, the principal of the Hitchin Academy for the Daughters of Gentlemen. 'No,' she said, 'I don't. I want to stay here and look after Miss Ruth. Mr Rosen has given me a place here with good wages and a nice room all of my own and what's more . . .'

'There's more?' queried Laura when the young Irish woman paused.

'Yes, Ma'am, there's more. I'm to be specially trained as a lady's maid at some place in London so that I can look after

Miss Ruth when she goes into Society!'

'Are you, indeed?'

'Yes, Ma'am, me a lady's maid, me!'

With that Bridie's attention was taken up by two of Ruth's London cousins who demanded the refilling of their tumblers from the jug she was carrying.

That evening after three tired by happy children had been put to bed, Laura and Barnabas sat back in a candlelit rose bower in their own small garden to talk over the recent events which had culminated in the afternoon's pleasantries.

'All's well that ends so well,' said Barnabas, 'but why Mr Rosen presented Pearson, Hilton and myself with gold cravat pins as we left is rather beyond me. We did so little in obtaining Ruth's release.'

'Mrs Pearson and I did even less yet we were both given brooches!'

'And very charming that are too! No, Bridie is the one who did most for him and Ruth and I'm glad he's done what he has done for her.'

'So am I but I see a complication there, my dear.'

'A complication? What, pray?'

'It's more who than what!'

'Who, then?'

'Constable Hilton! He's smitten with Bridie!'

'Is he now?'

'Yes, he is! Badly! A least half a dozen times this afternoon he went to her for lemonade with his eyes poppin' out of his head!'

'And Bridie? Is she smitten with him, do you think?'

Laura smiled. Her eyes sparkled in the candlelight. 'Smitten enough to warmly return his kiss when they parted this evening!'

'You saw the exchange?'

'Yes, my love, I did. It was made behind the bushes near the marquee!'

'But if this develops and she marries Hilton she won't be able to continue looking after Ruth, will she? You know what it's like being married to a police officer.'

'I certainly do, but I don't think Arthur Hilton will be a policeman for much longer!'

'Why not? Whyever not? He's said nothing to me about leaving the force.'

'He has to Sergeant Pearson according to his wife. Mr Rosen has offered him a very good post!'

'Whatever as?'

'He's a neat writer, isn't he?'

'Yes, very neat and good.'

'And a good speller?'

'Yes, excellent!'

'Well, Mr Rosen wants him to be his personal secretarial assistant. Apparently he was most impressed with HIlton when they were locked up together underneath the railway arch and he thinks he would be a useful young fellow to have on his staff! If he takes what is being offered and also lives at Three Gables there will be no problem in respect of Bridie and she can continue to look after Ruth.'

Barnabas laughed. 'You women! You and Mabel Pearson have got it all worked out, haven't you? All cut and dried to your satisfaction, you matchmaking pair! But maybe Arthur Hilton won't take the post and will carry on being a very good policeman!'

But Constable Hilton did resign from the force and six months after doing so he was married to Brigid Mahony in St. Mary's Church. Sergeant Pearson was the best man, the bride was given away by Mr David Rosen and Ruth Rosen made a pretty bridesmaid. Laura and Barnabas attended the ceremony and were present at the small reception held at the Cock Inn afterwards. At the conclusion of the wedding breakfast when they were watching the departure of the newlyweds in a carriage to commence their honeymoon Barnabas turned to Laura with a wry smile to murmur, 'There goes a man who would have made a good police sergeant, perhaps even a good inspector!'

Laura, looking up at him through the happy tears which always came to her eyes on romantic occasions, replied, 'But he's not going to, is he? Instead he's going to make a very nice girl a very nice husband and they're going to bring up a very nice family together, What better could you ask?'

'Nothing, my dear, nothing! Absolutely nothing!' said the tall inspector.

**The first Tripp crime novel is entitled The Tall Hitchin Sergeant and is available via any bookshop.**

In the autumn of 1858 Barnabas Tripp was promoted to the rank of sergeant and took post at the headquarters of the Second Division of the Hertfordshire Police, stationed at Hitchin.

There he soon found himself helping to cope with a crime wave in which the Devil was nearly raised, a royal train almost wrecked and two young girls were brutally murdered. He acquires a dog by the name of Benjy and among those he meets during his investigations are a woman poacher who is a deadly shot with a gun and a butcher who is equally deadly with a pole-axe.

He also finds romance with the lovely Laura Ashton and eventually marries her in Hitchin's great and beautiful church of St. Mary the Virgin, despite the intervention of the witchlike Zena Tavass on their wedding day.

# Books Published by THE BOOK CASTLE

**JOURNEYS INTO HERTFORDSHIRE:** Anthony Mackay.
Foreword by The Marquess of Salisbury, Hatfield House.
Nearly 200 superbly detailed ink drawings depict the towns, buildings and landscape of this still predominantly rural county.

**JOURNEYS INTO BEDFORDSHIRE:** Anthony Mackay.
Foreword by The Marquess of Tavistock, Woburn Abbey.
A lavish book of over 150 evocative ink drawings.

**COUNTRYSIDE CYCLING IN BEDFORDSHIRE,
BUCKINGHAMSHIRE AND HERTFORDSHIRE:** Mick Payne.
Twenty rides on- and off-road for all the family.

**LEAFING THROUGH LITERATURE:
Writers' Lives in Hertfordshire and Bedfordshire**: David Carroll.
Illustrated short biographies of many famous authors and their connections with these counties.

**THROUGH VISITORS' EYES: A Bedfordshire Anthology**:
edited by Simon Houfe.
Impressions of the county by famous visitors over the last four centuries, thematically arranged and illustrated with line drawings.

**THE HILL OF THE MARTYR:
An Architectural History of St. Albans Abbey**: Eileen Roberts.
Scholarly and readable chronological narrative history of Hertfordshire and Bedfordshire's famous cathedral. Fully illustrated with photographs and plans.

**LOCAL WALKS: South Bedfordshire and North Chilterns**:
Vaughan Basham. Twenty-seven thematic circular walks.

**LOCAL WALKS : North and Mid-Bedfordshire**: Vaughan Basham.
Twenty-five thematic circular walks.

**CHILTERN WALKS: Hertfordshire, Bedfordshire and
North Buckinghamshire**: Nick Moon.

**CHILTERN WALKS: Buckinghamshire**: Nick Moon.

**CHILTERN WALKS: Oxfordshire and West Buckinghamshire:**
Nick Moon. A trilogy of circular walks, in association with the Chiltern Society. Each volume contains thirty circular walks.

**OXFORDSHIRE WALKS: Oxford, the Cotswolds and
the Cherwell Valley**: Nick Moon.

**OXFORDSHIRE WALKS: Oxford, the Downs and
the Thames Valley**: Nick Moon.
Two volumes that complement Chiltern Walks: Oxfordshire and complete coverage of the county, in association with the Oxford Fieldpaths Society. Thirty circular walks in each.

**FOLK: Characters and Events in the History of Bedfordshire and
Northamptonshire**: Vivienne Evans. Anthology about people of yesteryear – arranged alphabetically by village or town.

**LEGACIES: Tales and Legends of Luton and the North Chilterns**:
Vic Lea. Twenty-five mysteries and stories based on fact, including Luton Town Football Club. Many photographs.

**ECHOES: Tales And Legends of Bedfordshire and Hertfordshire**:
Vic Lea. Thirty, compulsively retold historical incidents.

**MYTHS and WITCHES, PEOPLE and POLITICS:**
**Tales from Four Shires: Bucks., Beds., Herts., and Northants.**:
John Houghton.
Anthology of strange but true historical events.

**ECCENTRICS and VILLAINS, HAUNTINGS and HEROES.:**
**Tales from Four Shires: Northants., Beds., Bucks. and Herts.**:
John Houghton.
True incidents and curious events covering one thousand years.

**THE RAILWAY AGE IN BEDFORDSHIRE**: Fred Cockman.
Classic, illustrated account of early railway history.

**JOHN BUNYAN: HIS LIFE AND TIMES**: Vivienne Evans.
Foreword by the Bishop of Bedford. Preface by Terry Waite.
Bedfordshire's most famous son set in his seventeenth century context.

**SWANS IN MY KITCHEN: The Story of a Swan Sanctuary**:
Lis Dorer. Foreword by Dr Philip Burton. Updated edition.
Tales of her dedication to the survival of these beautiful birds through her sanctuary near Hemel Hempstead.

**WHIPSNADE WILD ANIMAL PARK: 'MY AFRICA'**: Lucy Pendar.
Foreword by Andrew Forbes. Introduction by Gerald Durrell.
Inside story of sixty years of the Park's animals and people – full of anecdotes, photographs and drawings.

**DUNSTABLE WITH THE PRIORY, 1100–1550**: Vivienne Evans.
Dramatic growth of Henry I's important new town around a major crossroads.

**DUNSTABLE DECADE: THE EIGHTIES: –**
**A Collection of Photographs**: Pat Lovering.
A souvenir book of nearly 300 pictures of people and events in the 1980s.

**DUNSTABLE IN DETAIL**: Nigel Benson.
A hundred of the town's buildings and features, plus town trail map.

**OLD DUNSTABLE**: Bill Twaddle.
A new edition of this collection of early photographs.

**BOURNE AND BRED: A Dunstable Boyhood Between the Wars:**
Colin Bourne.
An elegantly written, well-illustrated book capturing the spirit of the town over fifty years ago.

**ROYAL HOUGHTON**: Pat Lovering.
Illustrated history of Houghton Regis from the earliest times to the present.

**BEDFORDSHIRE'S YESTERYEARS Vol. 1: The Family,
Childhood and Schooldays:** Brenda Fraser-Newstead.
Unusual early 20th century reminiscences, with private photographs.

**BEDFORDSHIRE'S YESTERYEARS Vol 2: The Rural Scene:**
Brenda Fraser-Newstead.
Vivid first-hand accounts of country life two or three generations ago.

**THE CHANGING FACE OF LUTON: An Illustrated History:**
Stephen Bunker, Robin Holgate and Marian Nichols.
Luton's development from earliest times to the present busy
industrial town. Illustrated in colour and monochrome. The three
authors from Luton Museum are all experts in local history,
archaeology, crafts and social history.

**THE MEN WHO WORE STRAW HELMETS:
Policing Luton, 1840–1974:** Tom Madigan.
Meticulously chronicled history; dozens of rare photographs; author
served Luton Police for nearly fifty years.

**BETWEEN THE HILLS: The Story of Lilley, a Chiltern Village:**
Roy Pinnock.
A priceless piece of our heritage – the rural beauty remains but the
customs and way of life described here have largely disappeared.

**FARM OF MY CHILDHOOD, 1925–1947:** Mary Roberts.
An almost vanished lifestyle on a remote farm near Flitwick.

**THE TALL HITCHIN SERGEANT:
A Victorian Crime Novel based on fact:** Edgar Newman.
Mixes real police officers and authentic background with an exciting
storyline.

# SPECIALLY FOR CHILDREN

**VILLA BELOW THE KNOLLS: A Story of Roman Britain:**
Michael Dundrow.
An exciting adventure for young John in Totternhoe and Dunstable
two thousand years ago.

**ADVENTURE ON THE KNOLLS: A Story of Iron Age Britain:**
Michael Dundrow.
Excitement on Totternhoe Knolls as ten-year-old John finds himself
back in those dangerous times, confronting Julius Caesar and his army.

**THE RAVENS: One Boy Against the Might of Rome:** James Dyer.
On the Barton Hills and in the south-east of England as the men of
the great fort of Ravensburgh (near Hexton) confront the invaders.

Further titles are in preparation.
All the above are available via any bookshop, or from the
publisher and bookseller

**THE BOOK CASTLE
12 Church Street, Dunstable, Bedfordshire, LU5 4RU
Tel: (01582) 605670**